Praise *for* Tales of Love *&* Despair

"Based on her interviews with men who lived through the Iranian Revolution, the author delivers eight short stories that examine the human condition. Moving freely between past and present, these narratives pit the romantic idealism of youth against the sobering reality of growing up, growing old, and growing apart. These evocative stories artfully explore every facet of humanity ... an impressive collection about relationships in a turbulent Iran that offers powerful insights."
—Kirkus Reviews (Starred Review)

"In *Tales of Love and Despair*, sociologist Mahnaz Kousha draws from extensive interviews to craft eight short stories that capture the spirit of an era ... Set between the 1970s and 1990s, these clear accounts from seldom-heard voices explore relationships at different stages. From teenage devotion to courtship, from midlife resignation to the pain experienced by couples with conflicting ideals, marriages illuminate the strengths and flaws in every heart ... *Tales of Love and Despair* offers moving examples of personal struggles. With its multifaceted approach to love, the book transcends culture to speak to wider human experiences."
—Clarion Reviews (Four Star Review)

"Kousha is talented writer and storyteller. Her characters, grinding through a world they did not create and cannot escape, are believable and sympathetic. Ultimately, she demonstrates that there's much more to Iranian life than politicians and the media would have us believe. Students of contemporary history and politics—and anyone who appreciates nuanced writing—will enjoy reading Kousha's stories."
—BlueInk Review

"Mahnaz Kousha's new book, *Tales of Love and Despair*, presents eight compelling narratives of Iranian men struggling to find love and matrimonial happiness during the 1980s and 1990s. Based on extensive interviews the author conducted with the men, the very different experiences of each man falling in—and sometimes out of—love complicate our understanding of male gender attitudes and roles in one of the largest Muslim countries. These stories are real, not fiction, and collectively they contribute, albeit unintentionally, to the demolition of many stereotypes about Iran."

—Eric Hooglund, editor of *Middle East Critique*

"For decades now, Americans have seen mostly the public and political face of Iran, through the news media. Now, in these subtle and deeply moving short stories by Mahnaz Kousha, we are brought into the private spaces of Iranians during the period on either side of the revolution. The characters Kousha creates allow us to feel the lives of Iranians intimately. Through her steady voice and keen eye for detail, she helps us to understand a society that is quite different from our own, while also allowing us to feel the men and women who inhabit it are very much like ourselves, with similar needs, desires, and, yes, ordinary tragedies."

—Greg Hewett, author of *Blindsight*

"These sensitive portraits of not necessarily sensitive men provide a glimpse inside a forbidden city. Mahnaz Kousha's short stories explore the minds of people living in modern Tehran, and demonstrate the effects that regime changes and wars have on contemporary society. We see life doggedly carrying on after the revolution in Iran. We see resilience as well as sacrifices. We also see an admirable sense of duty and altruism among men and women. From a ground's eye-view, these stories reaffirm the indomitable human spirit."

—James Cihlar, author of *The Shadowgraph*

TALES OF LOVE
AND DESPAIR

TALES OF LOVE AND DESPAIR

Men In Love In Revolutionary Iran

MAHNAZ KOUSHA

The story "Where Are We? We Are Here" was initially published in *aaduna*, Vol. 7, No. 1, and is republished here with permission.

Cover and book design by Aydin & Navid Mohseni.

Library of Congress Cataloging in Publication Data
Mahnaz, Kousha.
      Tales of Love and Despair: Men in Love in Revolutionary Iran
LCN: 2017905554
ISBN-13: 978-1545080375
ISBN-10: 1545080372
BISAC: Fiction / Short Stories

10   9   8   7   6   5   4   3   2   1

To all the men
who made this book possible

Table *of* Contents

Foreword

When my sociological study, *Voices From Iran: The Changing Lives of Iranian Women,* was published by Syracuse University Press in 2002, I received many comments. The men who spoke to me insisted that I should also interview them because they saw their experiences very differently from those of the women. Men were portrayed through the stories of women. The men who talked to me felt silenced. Their voices were missing. Some even suspected the women's accounts, wondering if they had told the truth, or if I had represented them accurately. A common phrase was, "It wasn't like that in my family." On the men's insistence, I decided to interview men in the same way that I had the women, using the same method and same questions. I contacted several sources in Iran, family members and friends, to find men who were willing to speak to me regarding their life experiences and family relationships.

Completing the interviews took a few years. As I started to transcribe, translate, and summarize my findings, I found it difficult to write about the men. The accounts they shared had numerous gaps; gaps in expressing emotions, gaps in intimate relationships with their loved ones, gaps in details of their lives. I knew they shared more with me than if I were male. That's what most of them told me. They saw me more as a therapist or counselor than as a sociologist. I, however, found their silences potent, pregnant with deep-felt introspection and emotions. It felt as if they were wondering how much or what to share. Long moments of silence often broke down with expressing painful experiences such as spending years as a political prisoner, accused of disloyalty to the new regime or witnessing group execution of inmates.

Respecting their silences meant missing a coherent account. Faced with such gaps, I had no solution but to change genres to create room for untold details and suppressed emotions. I needed the freedom and permissiveness of fiction. Short stories became my choice. However, trained as a sociologist, I had never written fiction. I, therefore, immersed myself in the world of short stories. This was a new world to me, an unknown sea, full of mystery. I delved into a new genre after decades of teaching and writing sociology.

Each story is about one person whom I had interviewed. My goal was to remain true to the stories I had been told. I included certain social or historical details that made the protagonists' lives more vivid, more real, and more engaging for the reader. But I refrained from changing or adding imaginary details. I respected the men's stories. The sociologist in me wanted to stay as close as possible to the narrative they had shared. Whether or not the stories were truthful was not my concern. I was not an investigator, even though the multiple questions I asked revealed contradictions and discrepancies in the stories.

Although these stories belong mostly to the early years of the Iranian Revolution (1979), their significance has not faded. Narrative of shared love, failed marriages, shattered dreams, lost youth, sacrifice and forgiveness are common around the world. The men's accounts are colored by a revolution that dramatically changed the world of Iranians, but they still share much in common with other cultures and societies. My hope is for the reader to discover the commonality of experiences, even though their cultural contexts may be drastically different. The stories provide multiple journeys that I expect bring people closer across cultures and societies. For dramas of life are never ending, never experienced in isolation, though often silenced or suppressed.

As a last word, I would like to take the opportunity and thank those who have helped me throughout this experience. My sincere thanks go to Greg Hewett for the writing workshop we had, for encouraging me to continue working on these stories, for reading every one of them, and giving me precious advice. Our discussions helped me sharpen my ideas, trying to be not only a storyteller but a cultural interpreter as well. I am most grateful for his intellectual companionship, continuous encouragement, and selfless dedication of his time and his knowledge. Without his support, these stories would have remained in my drawer, finally to be thrown away.

I would also like to thank James Cihlar for his editorial guidance. His reading of the stories made me tackle vague notions, and taught me to read the stories from an American reader's perspective. My heart-felt thanks go also to Aydin Mohseni for his creative artwork and his enthusiasm to see this work published online. When I asked him if he could help me with publishing the stories online, his positive response made the world a kinder place. He managed to find enough time in the middle of his own demanding work to deliver these stories into your hands.

Much grateful acknowledgement goes to the men and women in Iran who helped me find men for my interview project. Finding men who were willing to be interviewed in a closed culture where suspicion of the others is common due to the political environment is not an easy task. Finally, my sincere thanks go to the men who agreed to be interviewed in spite of the cultural barriers that prevented them from talking about their feelings and intimate relationships.

Two Women

My heart is like a lute
Each chord crying with longing and pain.
My Beloved is watching me wrapped in silence
      Rumi, *Hidden Music*

"WHY HAVEN'T YOU had your bath this week?" Ismael asked his mother when he returned from his trip.

"I don't want anybody to bathe me," Fatima replied, sounding indignant.

Ismael didn't probe. Instead he asked tenderly, "Will you let me do it?"

Nodding her head, Fatima gave her eldest son permission to bathe her. For the next twelve years Ismael and his Aunt Parvin washed Fatima's body every Friday. They removed her clothes, shampooed her hair, applied henna once a month to cover the unruly gray hair, lathered her heavy, limp figure, and lifted her to dry her. As Ismael held her in his strong arms, Aunt Parvin put fresh rose-scented clothes on Fatima. Carrying her to the living room, Ismael softly placed his mother down on the cotton mattress, and sat on the floor cushion to drink a cool mint sherbet that his wife served them. Only then did a faint smile appear on Fatima's face.

Half-soaked and exhausted, they were all grateful that one more bath had been accomplished. And no god or prophet was angered at the sight of a son washing his mother's naked body, holding her in his arms like a child, averting his eyes.

"That's not proper," relatives whispered. "A son shouldn't bathe his mother, shouldn't touch her unclothed body."

"Bathing my mother doesn't have anything to do with what's right or wrong. With God or the prophet's sayings," Ismael countered. "I do what my mother wishes and that's all that matters." But his reply didn't silence the voices of the believers.

After Fatima's debilitating stroke left one side of her body paralyzed, her family couldn't afford to hire a nurse. Ismael willingly accepted the task of bathing her because for him no love was purer, more innocent than the love of a son for his mother, or a mother for her son.

"He has no guilt," his uncle proudly whispered to Aunt Parvin at the funeral when Ismael carried Fatima's body on his shoulder in a casket. "Everybody is crying their heart out, weeping and howling because they feel guilty. They know they abandoned her, failing to even bathe her properly. But not Ismael. No son has ever done so much for his mother."

§

Ismael's love for Fatima did not die with her passing from this world. He didn't need to go to the cemetery every Friday to wash her dusty tombstone, to sprinkle rosewater on the dry dirt, to bring fresh flowers, to pay the gang of beggar boys or wretched looking women clad in black chador who prayed for one's dead. Fatima lived on in his heart and in his mind. Every single flower of the damask rose bush in the yard reminded Ismael of his mother. He remembered the day Fatima brought the small potted plant home.

"Sweetheart, plant this rose in a nice sunny corner. You can use the crushed petals for rice pudding and other sweets. Put the rest in a pouch next to your clothes."

Another day, a small Queen of the Night jasmine plant was awaiting him when he got home.

"Leave your windows open at nights and take deep breaths. You'll never need a stronger love potion," Fatima told him.

People living down the street commented on the fragrance of the Night jasmine; it wasn't only Ismael who enjoyed the sweet, delightful scent. The entire neighborhood was out in the street in the evenings to take a deep breath. The sweet perfume washed out the daily pains, hurts, and angers. Total strangers smiled at each other as they walked by the house. The jasmine had an intoxicating impact on the passersby, and the neighborhood gradually came to be known as the Queen of the Night.

As Ismael sipped his morning tea, Fatima came to his mind—cutting a fragrant single flower from the rose bush, putting it by his teacup. Later, Ismael gave it to the first little girl he saw on the street, for that was what Fatima had always done.

§

As a child of a refugee family who had escaped Russia after the communist takeover in 1917, Fatima had learned to traverse two cultures and two languages from an early age. The elders in the extended family stayed glued to one another, feeling lucky to have escaped a godless government. But the arduous journey had exhausted their fire, weakened their spirit, leaving no energy to start over. They couldn't stop wondering about their life back in Tiflis, their belongings, and the loved ones who didn't leave in time. Their only hope was to go back, to not to die in a foreign land. The feeling of exile hurt. It would take the children of the next generation to adjust and adapt to the new culture.

It was Fatima's job to be the mediator, to play the translator for her parents who never learned to speak Farsi adequately. Growing up as the cultural ambassador, she learned to give freely, to care abundantly, for she had learned what it meant to live with a devastating sense of loss, with displacement and grief about the vanished past. If anybody needed a letter, she wrote it. If her mother went to the doctor, she accompanied her. If her uncle wanted to negotiate the increasing rent, Fatima stood next to him. If her younger cousins sought help with their homework, she was the one who tutored them. She became a problem solver, offering a hand no matter who was getting married or giving birth. If an aunt became ill, the family knew Fatima would send food and was willing to nurse the sick back to health.

It was Fatima who had raised a son who could give selflessly. Ismael had learned to love generously, abundantly, optimistically.

§

"But why, dear?" Fatima wanted to know when Ismael told her about enlisting in the military. "You have a good job, making good money," she said with despair in her voice.

"I have to go, Mother. There is a war and I want to serve my country."

"How can I take care of all the children by myself?" Fatima pleaded.

"The children are getting older and Father will be transferred. The railroad company has promised to place him in Tehran soon," Ismael consoled.

"Who knows when the transfer will happen? And you know when your father is in town he spends most of his time with his parents and friends," she said tearfully. "You've been like a father to your siblings. My sweet boy, I need you. I need you right here."

"It's too late, Mother. I've already volunteered. I can't take my word back. I have to go."

In her heart, Fatima knew why Ismael had decided to enlist. She had watched her son slowly turning into a man. It started with shaving his face every morning although he didn't yet have much facial hair. He took a clean shirt to the mechanic shop he worked at so he could change before leaving. Folding the shirt neatly, he put it under his mattress every night and by morning he had a pressed shirt. Fatima also noticed Ismael becoming more sensitive, more dreamy, spending long minutes in front of a small mirror in the bathroom. He was even reciting love poems, whispering love songs to himself. Although she noticed all these developments, she had decided to stay quiet about the reason for the sparkle in his dark black eyes, about the joyful smile printed on his lips even while he was sleep.

"He is only fifteen," she told herself when she first noticed that otherworldy look in his eyes. "In a year or two, he won't even remember this girl."

Fatima knew nobody would take a fifteen year-old boy seriously, no matter how deeply in love he was. But more than three years passed and Ismael's love was only getting stronger. Fatima felt sorry for her son, for his unrequited love.

Although Ismael was normally full of energy, recently Fatima had noticed his melancholic mood, as though he were engulfed in deep sorrow. The news of his enlistment shook her. Which was worse, being hopelessly in love or joining the military? Distraught by the turn of events, she turned to her mother for advice. The two women had lived together all their lives and neither could face the tragedy of losing Ismael; he was their first—the first son and the oldest grandson.

The grandmother pleaded with Ismael. "Dear, you don't yet know about the horrors of war." For the first time in her life, she told him about the suffering her family had endured in Russia, her frequent nightmares, leaving her elderly parents behind, taking only what she could carry.

She still grieved for the family that was left behind. "There is no glory in fighting. No one would ever forget the atrocities. You're my oldest grandson, my crown. Why do you want to fight in a war that has nothing to do with us?" she asked him quietly. "We haven't immigrated to this country, leaving everything behind, to lose our loved ones to another war. We are newcomers to this land; this is not our homeland. We didn't flee one government to become victims of another."

All to no avail. Like all men defeated in love, rejected by a beloved, Ismael was subsumed in his misery, unable to hear Fatima's cries or his grandmother's pleas. No word of wisdom worked. Disheartened and hopeless, humiliated and chastened, he volunteered to serve in the war of 1973, or the Dhufar War. Ismael had no idea what the fighting was about, or even who was fighting whom. At eighteen, he harbored no hope for the future, but he vividly remembered the Monday that changed his life forever.

§

In 1970 Ismael was fifteen and full of pride and adolescent joy. No worries clouded his days. No father to impose unreasonable discipline.

Ismael and his friend Jamal were part of a youth group preparing for the annual religious rituals. The procession required much planning, starting at one point of the neighborhood, marching a certain route, reaching a particular destination, perhaps a mosque or the house of a neighborhood dignitary that provided food for all the participants. Organizing the march was not to be taken lightly. No two processions should reach an intersection simultaneously because the encounter could end up in mayhem, with each troupe pressing to go. To pass the crossroad first was a sign of status, depicting the power of their professional guild and the strength of the neighborhood. Ultimately the procession that passed first demonstrated its superiority by making the other group delay their march forward. No man could afford to lose face; no procession was willing to be the second; therefore, organizing and navigating the route was crucial to save face for all the men involved.

It was in the middle of mapping the neighborhood, planning the route, designating strategic locations for water containers and cool sherbets that Ismael's eyes landed on the thirteen year-old Solmaz. She was dressed in a gray school uniform. Her hair pulled back in a bun accentuated her high cheekbones and large brown eyes. Her family had offered to provide iced water to the marching men, and Ismael and Jamal were delivering big buckets to their door to be filled and refilled for the day of the procession. Ismael became the self-designated watchman by her house. During the march, he made sure nobody loitered around Solmaz's house, throwing a secret look at the girls and women who watched the procession from behind the latticed windows of her house.

To the unaccustomed observer, the procession was a fearful and heart-rending religious ritual to mourn the murder of Imam Hossein thirteen centuries earlier. Those who march forcefully beat their chests, chanting religious verses. To the believers, the march represents unity with the Imam Hossein. Listening to the story of Imam Hossein's martyrdom and sacrifice creates a strong yearning for justice against tyranny. But to the untrained eye, and perhaps some adults, the procession carried other meanings as well. It was a rare occasion for the men to unbutton their black shirts, to bare their hairy chests, to showcase their masculinity. To exhibit religious passion and chant with their operatic voices was an extraordinary event. While the men fervently pounded their bare chests, women stood by the sidewalks or behind windows to watch.

As a little boy, Ismael heard young men quietly talking about fireworks during the procession, but he had never seen any. "Where are the fireworks?" he kept asking his tall, handsome uncle. Ismael had never seen any fire crackers during the annual procession.

"You'll find out for yourself. For now just follow our procession and make sure you don't get lost. Remember we live on Salsebil Street. If you got lost, just ask how to get to Salsebil, and people will show you the direction."

Ismael couldn't wait to find out what the young men meant by *fireworks*. Firmly grabbing his uncle's shirttail, Ismael tried to imitate the syncopated walk of the men, and sang from the bottom of his heart. While he had no idea what he was chanting, the verses the procession's leader ceaselessly recited and the rhythm of the lamentation were etched in his memory. Intuitively, he felt the vibrating energy that unconsciously shook him to his bones. He felt ecstatic, entranced by the chanting, by the explosive power of the excited crowd. Fatima kept telling him not to shout so much, for he always lost his voice by the time he went home. Although little boys were not supposed to beat their chest, Ismael pounded on his chest in imitation of the grown-ups.

§

The women's exclusion from marching and singing conferred on them an extraordinary power of scrutiny. Of gazing. While the men marched and sang religious hymns, Ismael came to see fireworks with his own eyes. Nobody needed to tell him to watch.

Women are like butterflies, he reflected. Watching closely, he saw some women moving their wings, gracefully parting their veils, seductively showing their necks and the stylish outfits they wore under their veils, and charmingly closing the veils to leave room for imagination. The men's eulogies to the long ago religious martyr gained more momentum with each benevolent undoing of the women's veil followed by its tactful enclosing. The processions brought the men and women to the streets, behind the latticed windows and half-open entryways, offering a deliciously sanctified occasion for the hungry eyes and eager hearts.

§

Waiting by Solmaz's house all day, seemingly to ensure the water containers remained full at all times, Ismael felt desperately sad when she didn't even come to the window to watch the procession. The next day he joined the group of boys who hung around the girls' schools. The romantic ones hungered for eye contact with their favorite girl; the brave ones followed them home, desperately trying to exchange a word or two, begging for an acknowledgment. The roughnecks were only eager to satisfy their ravenous eyes, not limiting themselves to one girl or one school.

Most girls saw these boys as losers. No reputable girl ever gave them the time of day, let alone cast a look toward them. They knew those boys had no prospects; furthermore, they didn't want to sully their future by being associated with such derelicts.

§

Ismael became a permanent fixture at Solmaz's school, standing by the door not too far from the pack of boys who gawked at the girls, whistling, calling them names, and showing off their irreverent budding masculinity. When the school door opened, the girls poured out of the drab building, lively and vivacious, their waves of energy reaching deep into the hearts of the lingering boys. Escorting Solmaz and her friends home—supposedly to protect them against roughnecks from other neighborhoods—gave Ismael a sense of manhood. All the boys knew Solmaz was his, and nobody dared so much as mention her name in his presence.

"He'll go away. Just ignore him," Solmaz's older sister Samira consoled her. "Don't pay him any attention. He is a bum." Embarrassed by Ismael's unsolicited attention, Solmaz felt angry and upset.

Desperate, Ismael resorted to writing love notes, trying to pass them to her as she walked home carrying her schoolbooks. No letter ever remained in her possession for more than a second. If one note successfully reached her hand, she'd instantaneously cast it away as if it were poisonous. "How does he dare?" Solmaz asked her sister, appalled by Ismael's vulgar behavior. The more persistence Ismael showed, the more offended she felt.

Ismael confided in Jamal. "She tosses my letters away as if they were trash."

"All the girls are like that," Jamal consoled his young buddy. "They never accept a note from a boy, but deep in their hearts they want him."

Ismael sought the help of the neighborhood gofer, Reza, who was trusted by everybody. Little Reza was welcomed into all houses; the housewives relied on him for errands.

"Reza, would you buy me a kilo of onions?" asked one woman if Reza walked by her open kitchen window. "I forgot to get them this morning."

"Reza, would you get me a box of Tide?" asked yet another.

Eleven year-old Reza was the trustworthy boy everybody liked; he knew who was well or recovering from sickness, who was expecting a baby, and who had out of town visitors. And he overheard that Solmaz was having difficulty writing an essay for her class.

"I have never traveled," Solmaz complained to Sanaz while Reza put a heavy watermelon on the kitchen floor for Solmaz's mother. "We have always lived in this neighborhood. My school is down the street. My uncles and aunts live on the same block. What do I know about traveling?"

"Our teacher gives us the most boring topics for the composition class. Would you write me an essay?" Solmaz begged her sister. "Please. You write so beautifully."

As Solmaz whined about her essay, her mother turned to Reza and said, "Reza, why don't you stay for lunch?" She never let Reza leave without eating something, no matter what time of the day it was.

"Thank you, but I have to go," Reza said hastily. "Mother is waiting for me and she won't eat till I get home."

"Okay, then take some dolma for your mother." Wrapping a few stuffed cabbages in a dish, she didn't listen to Reza's polite objections.

Before running home, Reza made sure he stopped by the mechanic shop.

"Write an essay, will you, about traveling," he yelled excitedly the moment he spotted Ismael at the shop. "I need it tomorrow."

Raising his head from under the car, Ismael looked dumbfounded. "What are you talking about?"

Kneeling down by Ismael, careful not to put his knees on the dirty floor, Reza looked down at Ismael who was stretched out on the garage floor as if he were on a cotton mattress. "If you write a nice essay, I'll take it to her. You have traveled with your father. Your grandparents left their home country. You know about traveling more than all of us. You should write her an essay." Reza didn't mention any names, for even mentioning Solmaz's name was disrespectful.

Slowly grasping Reza's secret plan, a thrilled smile appeared on Ismael's face. "I'll do it. I can write about traveling. It'll be ready tomorrow. I'll bring it to your house before school."

That night Ismael's eyes did not close. Staying up, he finished not only a composition on the benefits of traveling but also a lengthy love letter about the heartache, the agony he had experienced every day, and his desperate need to see Solmaz. Every paragraph started with the phrase, "You're like a rose," and ended with various verses from popular songs. Ending with a verse from Rumi, "My Beloved is watching me wrapped in silence," he neatly folded his three-page letter, concluding to himself that nobody had ever written a more impassioned one. Putting his letter with the essay in a sealed envelope, he gave the package to Reza early next morning before going to work. Spending the rest of the day engulfed in simultaneous joy and agony, Ismael couldn't concentrate on his work. Finally, leaving early, he went home to shower before showing up at his post by the school door.

He easily spotted Solmaz the moment she stepped out of the schoolyard, surrounded by her friends. They walk like a moving fortress, Ismael thought to himself. His eyes zoomed in on Solmaz's every move, wondering why her friends were acting like a team of bodyguards. He was dying for eye contact, for any simple kind gesture. He wanted to know how the essay went, if the teacher had called on her to read her composition aloud, what grade she had gotten. He wanted to know everything. And his letter—he had spilled his heart out.

One more block and she'd be home. And she hadn't even thrown a glance at him. He could tell she was aware of his presence, for he was following them closely, every step of the way.

They all know I am here, walking right behind them, he thought angrily. Ismael was baffled by the open hostility the girls showed. Then, watching Solmaz carefully, all of a sudden he felt euphoric. Solmaz was holding his envelope in her left hand, close to her heart. He was overjoyed by the gesture. Yes, she has finally accepted my love, he felt reassured.

The big smile on his face suddenly turned into utter shock as he watched Solmaz raise her hand nonchalantly and toss the package, while at the same time shooting him the most vindictive look. Her calm and composed move stabbed him in the chest. He stood, frozen. The envelope hit the trunk of a big old plane tree and fell heavily into the dirty running stream that ran beside the sidewalk. The packet was swallowed into the current immediately, only to be ejected a few meters away, wet but still sealed. The laughter of Solmaz's friends brought.

§

Solmaz's friends, especially Firoozeh, laughed for days about the horror-stricken look on Ismael's face, cracking jokes about his

13

disappearance. "He's gone mad, just like Majnun. You're his Layla," said Firoozeh mockingly.

"He will be forced to marry his ugly cousin," said another.

The girls figured he wouldn't show up for a few days anyway, but Ismael wasn't there the next week. Or the following weeks. Nobody knew of his whereabouts, as if he had vanished into thin air. One month, two months. The boy who had become a permanent fixture by the school door for more than two years, escorting them home, guarding them like a faithful dog, went missing. All he had ever done was wait for them by the school door, write love notes, and unsuccessfully try to pass them on to Solmaz.

Firoozeh, who was particularly infuriated by Ismael's annoying presence, said, "Thank goodness, we don't have to see his face anymore."

But Safa said, "Well, it wasn't that bad to have him escort us home. At least we didn't have to deal with those other boys."

"We shouldn't be dealing with any of them," Firoozeh said angrily. "They have no right loitering at the school gawking at us like that."

"Oh, they don't mean any harm. They are just boys who don't know what to do with themselves," Safa countered.

"They can get a job to help their parents. They're harassing us all the time and we can't even tell our parents because a fight might break out. I don't want my father or brother to ever talk to those derelicts."

Safa had a different view on the loitering boys. "Listen, most of them live in tiny apartments. The poor boys don't have anywhere to go. They idle away their time on the block for a few years, but they'll find a job sooner or later. Actually, they'd protect you if a boy from another neighborhood ever looked at you." Safa didn't tell them that her own cousin was one of them.

"Yes, and in the meantime, I have to accept their disgusting gawking every day. No, thank you. I don't need their protection."

Complaining about the other boys was in fact a way to reminisce about Ismael without mentioning his name. Instead of feeling relieved for getting rid of Ismael, most of Solmaz's friends, except Firoozeh, started missing him. Safa was right: he had kept the others away. Nobody dared approach Solmaz and her friends because they feared Ismael's retribution. With Ismael out of the picture, other boys were acting like hungry wolves again, their predatory eyes feasting on the girls like easy prey.

If Ismael slowly became a distant memory for most of the girls, he remained very present in Solmaz's mind. She didn't miss him, but she did wonder about what had happened to him. Had she been so mean to drive him away completely? Throwing the envelope in the running stream was Firoozeh's idea. Embarrassed and angry by his incessant attention, Solmaz hadn't thought twice about Firoozeh's suggestion. But seeing the mortified look on his face had immediately made her realize the cruelty of her act. Solmaz wasn't a mean girl, and she didn't want to think that she'd caused Ismael's disappearance.

What about his mother, his family? Does anybody know where he is? Solmaz asked herself. She couldn't bring herself to ask Reza, but her eyes began seeking him at the end of the school day, imagining him at the same corner she had avoided looking at for more than two years. The same spot where a dandelion had always grown from a sidewalk crack. She found herself walking by the school, slowing down her steps to pick the yellow dandelion.

Why hadn't she read even one of his letters? She now regretted it.

§

And the rumors started.

"Ismael is in prison," the grocer told Firoozeh's mother.

"He's gone to Kuwait," the shoemaker volunteered. "Everybody is going to Kuwait to make money these days."

"He'll come back a rich man," the dry cleaning owner concluded.

But Solmaz overheard Reza as he was helping her mother. "Mr. Vahabi's son has joined the military. And he's volunteered to serve in the war."

What war? Solmaz asked herself silently as she heard her mother asking the same exact question aloud.

The next day Solmaz asked her friends if they knew there was a war.

"A war?" the girls asked in unison.

"You don't know what's happening in our own country?" Firoozeh said with her usual tone of superiority. "It's in the papers. The Dhufar War. The Shah is sending troops to protect the kingdom of Oman."

Looking at each other in bafflement, nobody said anything. They didn't know what to think. Unlike their parents and grandparents who had seen the devastating impact of the First and Second World Wars, as well as the 1950s CIA coup in Iran, these girls lived their lives behind a veneer of political tranquility and couldn't imagine what war meant. They were taught by their parents to never ever talk politics, to always turn a deaf ear and walk away from anybody who mentioned anything about the government.

"Anyone could be a secret agent," they were warned by their parents. "A Savaki." The word delivered a chill to their hearts. They learned not to pursue the issue further.

That very day, Solmaz left home in the early evening to buy the daily newspaper for the first time in her life. Nobody read the paper in her home; sometimes she picked up a bit of news if her mother left the radio on to listen to music. Inspecting the headlines, the war news was right on the front page. Walking slowly, she scanned the article: *...sending forces... Oman ... Sultan Ghaboos... Yemeni attack.*

Where was Oman, she wondered. They weren't taught about Arab countries in school. She knew about Europe and the French Revolution, Napoleon Bonaparte and Queen Victoria, but nothing about Oman or Yemen.

Continuing to read, she found out that Sultan Ghaboos was facing an armed communist insurgency. Iran, Jordan, and England were helping the newly established government to fight the rebels.

Staring at the page blankly, she wondered what an armed communist insurgency was. They weren't taught about communism in school. It was a hushed word, only whispered here and there. What was an insurgency? She had no clue. She didn't see why the Shah should send troops to another country, and what all this meant to her.

Taking the news in, she felt acutely conscious of her surroundings, the busy-looking passersby, the few men standing at the bakery, the quiet vegetable and fruit vendors with their late evening customers. The mechanic shop and dry cleaning stores were the last stops for the men to exchange the most recent gossips or to throw lascivious looks at the neighborhood girls and the women who were out running their last errands. Avoiding eye contact with the men standing idly at the mechanic shop, Solmaz focused on the children who were playing soccer in the street, screaming joyfully.

Life didn't seem any different. She finally decided that the war couldn't be that important if everybody was living their life as usual. Nobody looked worried or concerned.

Maybe Ismael has really left for Kuwait, she contemplated. She didn't see any point in tormenting herself over a rumor.

Besides, she hadn't done anything wrong, Solmaz assured herself, trying to remember how annoyed she was by Ismael's persistent presence at the school. How embarrassed she'd felt in front of her friends. Even if he were in the military, that wasn't her fault. He had decided to volunteer on his own.

But the rumors turned into a torrent of stories as the daily papers wrote about the war. The Shah was committed to sending several units with their own helicopters to assist Sultan Ghaboos' forces against the communists.

If newspapers wrote about the army, Reza delivered news about Ismael. By then everybody knew what Ismael had done.

§

Underestimating Ismael's love for that girl had proven to be a devastating mistake for Fatima. After the first initial phone calls home, Ismael stopped calling her. No word from him. No letters like he had promised. Weeks turned into months, and Fatima did not hear from her son. He had completely disappeared. Every time Fatima went to the military office, she was told her son was all right because he was on the payroll. Begging to know his whereabouts, she was always given a vague reply. She finally went to the military headquarters. As she cried and begged, she was sent from office to office, having to wait two hours here, half an hour there, only to hear the same unhelpful responses. Feeling at a total loss, one day she sat on the floor in a corner of the second floor hallway, following the officers with her tearful gaze as they paraded in their distinguished military uniforms. It was only then that a lieutenant took pity on her—perhaps because she reminded him of his own mother—asking her what she needed.

"I want to know where my son is, sir. His name is Ismael Vahabi. I haven't heard from him in a long time," she managed to say, trying hard to hold back her sobs.

"I'll see what I can do, mother," the sergeant said. "Stay right here, and don't go anywhere."

Fatima didn't remember how many times she counted the number of tiles on the floor, the dotted yellow ones and then the gray ones. How many had cracks and were chipped. She couldn't recall how many prayers she quietly recited. There were a couple of wooden benches for the visitors, but she didn't move to sit on them even when the floor became too hard, too cold. The benches were for more distinguished people. Finally the young officer who had accompanied the lieutenant returned.

"Your son is with the third unit that is stationed in the south," he reported.

"Sir, may I ask you where he is sent?" she asked thankfully. Apologetically.

"We can't reveal their location, but they'll be in Abadan for a few days before leaving."

"Where in Abadan?"

Shrugging his shoulders, he turned to leave. "A camp in the dessert."

§

Watching his wife put a shirt in a small plastic bag, Mr. Vahabi asked Fatima, "Where are you going?"

"Looking for my son," Fatima said calmly.

"You don't even know where he is," he responded angrily.

"I know where he is," Fatima replied, still maintaining her calm composure. "He is in Abadan. A kind officer told me."

"And you trusted him! Where the hell in Abadan, anyway? We don't know anybody there. They're all Arab. They don't even speak Farsi," Ismael's father continued. "You think Ismael is a child. First, you rent his room—"

Interrupting her husband in the middle of his sentence, Fatima snapped angrily. "He has worked since he was twelve. I want him to have some savings when he returns."

"We have given him everything," Ismael's father retorted.

"What have we given him? All the other boys have spending money. We've never given him anything to spend on his own. Ismael is the one who has brought us money," Fatima cried.

"He's in the army, taken care of, and paid a good salary," Mr. Vahabi persisted.

"I am the one who should take care of my son, not the army. I should provide for him."

"There is a war in Abadan. That's no place for a woman to go," he shouted. "I forbid you to go."

Boarders had come and stayed in spite of Mr. Vahabi's persistent objections. Neither the rumors about boarding strangers nor his protests made any difference to Fatima.

"She has young unmarried daughters at home," neighbors said.

"How dare she bring young men into her house?" her in-laws said reproachfully.

"I'll go as far as I can, as long as my legs carry my weight. I'll find my son no matter where he is, and I'll bring him back home." Those were Fatima's final words to herself.

Leaving her four children with her elderly mother, she said, "I won't be back until I find my Ismael." Nobody heard the door closing softly the next morning.

§

Ismael heard a familiar voice in his nightmarish stupor. Taking refuge in his tent from the blazing midday sun, he was grateful he wasn't sent to bring supplies from the nearest village. The unbearable heat caused momentary states of unconsciousness and hallucination, as though he were stuck in purgatory. The same voice reached him again. Opening his heavy eyes with much effort, he looked for his tent mates, four other eighteen year-old boys. Like him, none had finished high school, and all were from poor families.

"I am looking for my son, Ismael. He is a tall man." The voice echoed in his ears. Closing his eyes, he tried to focus, to shake himself out of his delusional state.

"Do you know him?"

Was this his imagination?

"You mean Ismael Vahabi?" asked the young guard who barely looked eighteen. Shocked to see a woman in their temporary quarters, he continued, "No, he isn't here. They left this morning to get supplies and haven't come back yet."

Ismael heard the soldier's worried voice, "You shouldn't stay here, mother. This is a war zone."

"It's all right, young man. I am coming from Tehran and have no place to go. It has taken me three days to find the troops. Nobody was willing to drive me this far; I have been walking since early morning. I'll wait right here for my son. For my Ismael."

The determined words, the voice heavy with grief and haunting pauses brought Ismael to jump from his thin mattress, almost tripping over in the small tent before rushing out.

"No, I am here, right here, Mother," Ismael shouted. "I didn't go with the others this morning."

Ismael knew that his mother was an exceptional woman, raising her five children almost alone, taking care of her entire family all by herself. But he had never imagined she'd come this far to find him.

The boy who had written love letter after love letter for Solmaz hadn't sent a word home for thirteen months.

§

"I go to sleep dreaming about her, Mother, and I wake up with her name," Ismael confessed feverishly to Fatima. "I don't even know how many times I've repeated her name; her name is my prayer. Hearing her name gives me strength, while at the same time stabbing me in the heart, right here," he pointed to his sunburned chest. "She is with me all the time, right by my side."

Months of keeping silent brought an explosion of tormented feelings. Though it wasn't manly to show weakness, to talk about his pain, Ismael could no longer keep quiet.

Fatima followed Ismael's fixed gaze on the empty and forbidding desert. Now that she was sitting next to her son, she felt one with him. Looking at the sun getting smaller by the minute, Fatima held Ismael's hand in her white, calloused grip, caressing his skin. His fingernails were no longer blackened and greased with the oil of the mechanic shop, but his skin felt coarse, like sandpaper.

Drawing his breath in, Ismael said, "I volunteered to serve on the front, hoping to die. I am not dead yet, but I live the life of a dead man."

Tenderly caressing his back, she could easily feel his bones protruding. Fatima remained quiet, not interrupting Ismael's tormented thoughts, for she knew no words could heal his heart.

Ismael continued in a hoarse whisper. "I can't get her out of my mind. I was happy to just walk behind her in the streets, watching out for her. Merely seeing her gave me joy. I was so sad on weekends because I didn't see her. She never left the house alone for an idle walk like the other girls. A kindhearted soul—that's what she is, always taking care of her nieces and nephews, taking them out for an ice cream while she never got any for herself. You could tell the children loved her dearly, competing with each other to hold her hand. Never looking right or left, never smiling at strangers. She is such a virtuous girl, I am sure she has never talked to a boy; I want a girl like that."

Fatima watched the desert sun turn into flaming red, then orange. Shielding her eyes against the sun, she could see the heat waves waltzing along the desert. The desert seemed to extend to eternity. No clouds, no objects obstructing her horizon.

That night Fatima and Ismael slept under the dark blue desert sky. While Ismael slept soundly for the first time in a long time, Fatima wondered about her son's broken heart that had sunk him into despair and caused him to prefer death to life. She wanted to give him back the joy of life. Giving birth to her baby son was one thing, protecting him against unrequited love was another thing entirely. Looking up, she saw moonlight illuminating the tents, her son's sleeping body, her thoughts.

With nothing protecting them against the early sunrise and the harsh bright sky, the mother and son woke and shared the dates Fatima carried with her.

"Don't worry, dearest," she said. "Everything will work out. Have faith. Just promise me to come home for a visit. You haven't taken any furloughs for a year and a half. It's time for you to visit the family. Everybody is worried about you."

Opening her crumpled collar, she reached deep into her shirt under her veil and pulled out her pouch. "This is yours," folding Ismael's big hand over a bundle of wrinkled and sweaty notes wrapped securely in a square plaid cloth. "You have more back home," Fatima said with a secretive smile.

"How come, Mother?" Ismael asked. "I should have sent you money to help with the expenses."

"I have been renting your room. Your grandparents are staying in one room, and the children and I sleep in my room. This is for you, dearest." Ismael was speechless, for he knew Fatima never had enough money even for their daily expenses.

Kissing him on his forehead, Fatima held her son's hand, whispering, "God willing, all will be well. You come home soon. Your family is anxious to see you, counting the days. Come home, my dear, and brighten up our days. Make us happy again."

§

Fatima had to devise a plan. She had heard that Solmaz was finishing high school and was planning to go to college. All her sisters had some kind of higher education and gotten good jobs. Ismael didn't even have his high school diploma. Marrying Ismael would certainly be a step down for Solmaz, and her parents wouldn't allow that. It would be bad for the rest of the girls in the family. Putting herself in their position, Fatima wondered who'd want to marry off their precious young daughter to a poor, high school dropout.

Have faith, she told herself. Ismael joined the army, volunteered to serve in the war only because Solmaz had rejected him. Believing in the power of empathy, she thought no young girl could overlook such a selfless love. No decent girl could bear the guilt of a young man dying on her account. He had put everything on the line for her. What else could a girl want in a husband? Listening to love songs on the radio, Fatima always wondered what the poets were talking about. Life had proven to be only a series of obligations and responsibilities. Mystery, perhaps even a hollow dream—that's what love was to Fatima, but now her son was infatuated with this girl, losing his sanity, willing to look death in the eye, forgetting the motherly love she had showered him with all his life.

To give him a second life, Fatima had no option but to try.

§

It wasn't her husband she consulted upon her return. Rather it was her women folk—mother, younger sister Jamila, a neighborhood friend Zari, and her aunt Parvin whose husband had left her with two children. Disappearing like a drop of water, he had never let the poor woman know his whereabouts.

All the women except Ismael's grandmother listened patiently to Fatima as she related her visit with Ismael. But the grandmother kept interrupting Fatima, going back and forth between prayers and curses interchangeably. "This girl has put a spell on my grandson," were the first words she uttered vindictively. "She should be honored to marry my Ismael."

"I wish my husband loved me like that," Zari said regretfully. "Love is the stuff of poetry."

Zari had found out about her husband's alcoholism only after marriage, resenting the fact that she frequently had to prepare food for him and his drinking buddies—which was more often than she could stand. "Men talk about love all the time, but they love their drink more than anything else. Once they have you, they want you as a maid, and pretty soon you find out they're more interested in other women. They don't even leave their friends' wives alone."

"Yes, I know. I know," Fatima said impatiently. "We know about men, but we are talking about my Ismael. Not other men. How can I even go and ask for this girl's hand when we are poorer than her family?"

Aunt Parvin said, "You're better off telling him to forget this girl. Keep your head up, and don't cause any embarrassment in the neighborhood and among relatives by asking for her hand." Although diplomacy wasn't one of her traits, Aunt Parvin nevertheless paused to weigh the impact of her next words. "I love my nephew, but you know he doesn't even have a chance. This family isn't going to marry off their daughter to your Ismael."

Exasperated, Fatima looked at her sister Jamila. Her pleading look said more than her words. Coming to her aid, Jamila said, "We may lose

Ismael if we don't do anything. We have to act and get to work fast before Ismael comes home for a visit."

"But what can we do?" Aunt Parvin asked impatiently.

"Talk to her friends," Jamila said resolutely.

"Whose friends?" asked Zari, still preoccupied in her forlorn thoughts.

Without paying attention to Zari, Jamila continued, "We need to find out who is in this girl's class. Who her best friends are. Tell them to put a good word for Ismael. She should know he's dead serious about her. She can't say no when she hears that he still wants her. This boy is willing to die because she has rejected him."

Pausing for a few seconds, Jamila said in a macabre tone, "She should know his blood is on her hands if she doesn't accept him."

The women looked at Jamila in astonishment, taken aback by her intensity, but Fatima seemed pleased.

§

The grandmother, however, had her own solution in mind, and she got to work fast. Taking her fourteen year-old grandchild with her to better navigate the busy streets, she went straight to the grand bazaar to visit the old potion-maker.

"My grandson needs help," she told him, sitting on a rickety stool by his counter. "Give me the strongest love cure you have."

To make sure his magic worked, she bought extra ingredients to concoct her own secret potion to sprinkle around Solmaz's house. For the next seven days, she went to Solmaz's home right at six in the morning to scatter the potion. She even placed a small but securely wrapped pouch on the dusty latticed window that opened to their kitchen window. Nobody would notice that because she covered it with old dry leaves.

The other women went to work also, casually talking to neighbors, friends, and shop owners. Jamila's friends were particularly helpful because their daughters attended the same school as Solmaz. Aunt Parvin came up with the wonderful idea of recruiting Ismael's friends who had young sisters. Everybody wanted to help. An entire network of women started talking about Mr. Vahabi's son who volunteered to serve in the war because the girl he loved had rejected him. Soon the daily suffering Ismael endured became the neighborhood's favorite tale of love and anguish.

"Who needs Ferdowsi or Nezami's epic love stories?" Jamila said to Fatima one day as she related overhearing street-corner boys talk about Ismael's love.

"We have our own Samson and Delilah, and Shireen and Farhad."

Fatima did her own part, telling stories about her grueling trip, the war she hadn't seen, the unbearable living conditions of the soldiers, the terribly high temperatures of the desert, and the sandstorms she had always heard about but never before experienced. Fatima became the neighborhood war correspondent. If anybody read a story in the evening newspaper, the facts were checked with her.

"Are the British Royal Forces involved?" asked an old neighbor who had vivid but bitter memories of British control.

"Yes, I saw them with my own eyes," Fatima reported confidently.

"Those British are everywhere," the neighbor said angrily. "They've always controlled our countries, telling us how to run our governments."

"But they are fighting the infidels this time."

"The newspaper says Jordan has sent troops too. Is that true?" another neighbor asked Fatima.

"Who are we fighting there?" the vegetable vendor asked Fatima when she walked by his shop. He had three sons, but he didn't want them to fight in any war he hadn't started.

"We are fighting the infidels."

Fatima had come to enjoy repeating the word "the infidels."

"There are some mean people out there," she reported with much authority. "Our boys are brave soldiers," she continued, shaking her head gravely, "but I'd do anything to bring my Ismael back home. A desert is no place to live."

Slowly Fatima came to claim the new role she had acquired in the neighborhood. Everybody was curious about the war; people delivered news to her personally, checking in with her to make sure their information was accurate. Having proven that she was a heroic mother, traveling all alone to the South, which was practically like a foreign country, Fatima had become a voice people trusted.

Rumor had it that she'd gone as far as the front where no civilian was permitted and found her son's brigade. Returning successfully was an absolute victory.

"You know her husband didn't want her to go, but she left anyway, carrying only a little money with her." The neighborhood women praised Fatima's heroism.

"I would have done the same thing if my husband wanted to stop me from looking for my son," they told themselves conceitedly.

§

By the time Ismael used his furlough to visit the family, the entire neighborhood knew that the Shah of Iran had sent a brigade of 1,200 forces to Oman to help the young Sultan Ghaboos in a coup against his father. While the deposed Sultan went into exile in London, the young Sultan was threatened by old adversaries aided by China.

Ismael came back as a quiet man, looking older and thinner. The lines in his face appeared deep, his look no longer that of a boyish eighteen-year-old. Welcomed enthusiastically by his own family, embraced wholeheartedly by the men and children, kissed by all the women relatives, treated like a war hero by neighbors and relatives, he wasted no time. The next day he was at Solmaz's school, cleanly shaven, sporting a nicely pressed plaid shirt Fatima had bought for him. Impatiently waiting for the school to let the girls out, his heart beat rapidly the moment he spotted Solmaz and her circle of friends.

"A pack of mean guard dogs," he reflected bitterly on his last encounter with them.

Taking a deep breath, he relaxed his shoulders as he zoomed in on her, his gaze as hot and penetrating as the desert sun he'd felt on his back. Moving resolutely toward them, he knew nothing would hold him back this time, but he was surprised to see that all of a sudden Solmaz's friends drifted away like autumn leaves as he neared. Only a couple slowed down, discretely keeping a reasonable space to allow enough room for the two of them to come together—but close enough to close in on him in case Solmaz needed help.

Finding himself face to face with Solmaz, with no protective human shield obstructing him, Ismael was speechless. But then, a bashful smile from Solmaz gave him heart. Without a word, they started walking next to each other.

Ismael didn't reach out for her hand for that was absolutely improper. A spell surrounded them in the middle of the busy sidewalk, accompanying them home. Engulfed in joy, Ismael knew nothing would ever again separate them. The long heart-wrenching speech he'd prepared remained within his heart, for they only spoke of love on the days that followed, of a future together. Solmaz posed no demands; she was now as determined as Ismael had ever been.

§

"Mother, I need a navy blue uniform and matching socks for school," Ismael's fifteen-year-old sister informed Fatima.

"Dear, Solmaz knows best about these things. Why don't you ask her to take you shopping," Fatima replied kindly.

"Mother, it's Teachers Day, and we're thinking about getting a present for Mrs. Minavi. What should we get?"

"Solmaz knows best. Ask her what you should get for your teacher."

After Ismael's younger brother Javad told his mother about the girl he wanted to marry, Fatima asked Solmaz to be in charge, to meet the family, and to arrange everything as she saw proper. Fatima visited the family only after Solmaz had approved the new bride, reporting back to Fatima that the girl seemed like a good match for Javad.

When Ismael's sisters fell in love with the neighborhood boys, they told Solmaz first. If they wanted to choose a field of study or look for a job, they consulted Solmaz. If Fatima had been the woman everybody consulted, she now willingly relegated that role to Solmaz. While Fatima didn't have enough money to provide necessities for Solmaz, now she willingly conferred to her all the power she had gradually acquired in her relations. Solmaz became an older sister to Ismael's siblings, a confidant, an intermediary, a marriage broker, a problem solver.

When they failed to have children within the first couple of years, to quiet the hurtful whispers Ismael confessed to his family that he was the source of the problem. Fatima consoled her son while trying to hush the wounding words.

"He loves this girl so much, he is willing to lie, to tell everybody that it's his fault," Ismael's grandmother said angrily. "This boy has no sense. He'd do anything for his bride. We've never had this kind of problem in our family."

"Mother, they're young. God willing they'll have many children when they're ready," Fatima would say consolingly, trying not to insult her elderly mother.

"I want to see my grandchildren before I die. I don't have much time left. If they don't have children soon, we should get another wife for Ismael."

"Mother, they're all right. Even if there is a problem, we can seek help from doctors. Nowadays they can cure anything. Even fifty year-old women are having children," Fatima assured her aging mother.

"I don't have that much time." Nothing could relieve the vexed grandmother. "I am going to the potion-maker; my grandson is jinxed."

The potion-maker was the grandmother's last resort for all kinds of problems.

Fatima's consoling words barely calmed her own doubts and worries down. What if her son really couldn't have children? She had to console Ismael, hide her own feelings by burying her painful doubts, and hush the hurtful gossip.

The woman who had returned victorious from a daunting journey to find her forlorn, love-struck son in the middle of the desert, was losing confidence in the face of family gossip.

But Fatima trusted God, the same God who had held her hand, had given her the courage to find Ismael and to bring him back to life. Or maybe the potion worked this time, for Ismael and Solmaz finally had their first of four children after five years.

With time, Solmaz's house became a sanctuary for children and adults alike. Returning home after the end of his workday, Ismael didn't know how many children would be in his yard, playing hide and seek, and screaming from the bottom of their hearts. Their house became a summer camp and a winter library; relatives wouldn't bother to find out about their children's whereabouts as long as they stayed at Aunt Solmaz's. No decisions were ever made without Solmaz's consultation, without her blessing.

Over time, Fatima's and Solmaz's roles blended. It was not clear where Fatima stopped and Solmaz started. They became one woman in two bodies.

§

Easing himself down into the deep hole the grave digger had made, Ismael raised his arms to collect Fatima's body. He had insisted on putting her in the ground himself. Once he softly rested her body wrapped in white cloth on the hot orange dirt, he removed the top part of the cloth slightly to have a last look at Fatima's face. Softly folding the cloth back over her wrinkled white skin, he looked up searching for Solmaz who handed him a few branches of the Jasmine of the Night in full bloom.

Where Are We?
We Are Here

ALI WAS RIDING home on the bus after two months of living in a tent at the mining site. He loved his job, the desert, and being with nature. The desert gave him an awareness of hidden life, invisible to the human eye. He felt its expansion and contraction, its breathing in and out.

Mining was his first choice of major when he took the university entrance exam, and he was ecstatic when he got accepted. That was in the early 1970s, when he was not yet twenty. Now in his early fifties, he still made regular trips to different mining sites. He listened to the humming of the engine, and felt the bus wheels turning around and around, carrying not only the weight of the bus itself, but the passengers and their belongings, their thoughts. He was carrying a heavy weight too, the burden of forgotten dreams and a marriage that he wanted to end after twenty-three years.

Seven more hours of riding and he'd be home, able to take a shower, and sleep on a soft bed. The other passengers were asleep; the only noise: an infrequent muffled cough, a whisper from the front, or the hum of the engine. Looking out the window, the absolute darkness of the night felt ominous. Ali fought sleep; he wanted to use the time to plan, to think about his projects, his life, and Mariam—who had no idea he was coming home.

§

The key chain in his pocket made a jangling noise with every step he took, but he didn't use it to open the door. He preferred to ring the doorbell and be greeted by the smiling face of his youngest son, Hamid, who always looked so delighted to see him. He was the self-designated butler. The expression on Hamid's face was what Ali looked forward to upon his return.

Grabbing his father's suitcase, Hamid leaned forward to kiss him on the cheeks, while hollering to his mother and older brother Jamshid, "Dad's here! He's home!" Ali hadn't called Mariam from the bus station to let them know he'd be home shortly. He knew his boys would be home; Mariam would also be back from her part-time work by five o'clock, perhaps in the middle of her daily phone conversation with her mother, Azizah.

Holding the phone in her hand, Mariam walked to the door. Taken aback to see him, her first words were, "You're back! Why didn't you call to let me know you'd be home?"

He smiled, not wanting to remark that he knew the phone would be busy. Mariam looked uncomfortable, thrown off, as though she were caught doing something wrong. She abruptly ended her phone conversation, not knowing exactly what to do now.

The boys were encircling Ali, greeting him with much noise. As they entered the living room, Mariam finally said, "I was planning to have leftovers tonight. Shall I cook something for dinner?" Looking perplexed, she automatically added, "But it's too late to start cooking."

She always appeared uptight the first few days Ali was back; it was as if an alien had invaded her space and she was no longer living with her own family in her own home.

"Boys, I'm going to take a shower," Ali announced to his sons. Looking toward Mariam, he added, "Leftovers are perfect. Anything is better than what I've been eating the last two months."

§

Hamid carried Ali's dusty suitcase to the laundry area, trying to separate the clean and dirty clothes, looking for the sweets his father brought every time he came back from a trip. Mariam was happy to see him unpacking the dirty suitcase, but she could not stop herself from saying, "Leave it there till I get a chance to wipe it down. Don't bring that dirty suitcase here." In the same breath, she told Jamshid to make some fresh tea for his father. "I'll get dinner ready soon."

As she followed Ali, she continued, sounding a little annoyed, "If I'd known you'd be back tonight, I would have cooked something for you." And in the next breath she asked, "When do you have to return to the site?"

That was always one of the first questions Mariam asked when Ali returned from his mining trips, and he increasingly resented it. He never really knew when the next problem would arise at the site. One phone call might send him packing his suitcase. It could be next week or three months later.

He wondered why Mariam never failed to ask that question before he even had enough time to change his dusty clothes. One minute. Two minutes. He would count the seconds before Mariam threw her question at him. There were things he had never understood about her. All that had initially attracted him had turned into a source of frustration, and then anger. He had been fascinated by her, but all his admiration slowly turned into a gradual disappointment and overall bitterness. He was no longer angry; he had simply given up—his disillusionment had been submerged into a deep sense of resignation.

Ali felt sorry for Mariam. He knew she was not happy with him either, but he was sorrier for himself. This was not the kind of marriage he had dreamed of. He gravely regretted his naïve decision to marry Mariam after they were both released from prison.

§

They knew each other more than six years before their marriage, but for all of that period one or the other was incarcerated. They met in prison and fell in love with bars between them. Ali was serving his term for supposedly participating in student demonstrations against the Shah. Mariam came with her mother to visit her brother Reza, another student. The two men were cellmates. Of all the romantic places the young could meet, Ali and Mariam had met in prison, and exchanged their first bashful glances in the noisy, tearful, daunting visiting room.

During his period of incarceration, Ali found himself dreaming about Mariam, building a life with her, buying a nice little home, having three children, a daughter for sure; he always wanted to have a little girl, to walk hand in hand with her in the park. It was that dream that kept him going, the shy glances they exchanged, careful that the guards did not suspect anything amorous between an unrelated man and woman, a prisoner and a visitor. It was this secret affair, strengthened with political passion, that gave Ali hope and a reason to bear his prison term.

Mariam accompanied Azizah every time to visit her brother. Her mother knew that the prisoners shared everything they had, and as far as she was concerned, if her son was innocent, all the prisoners were innocent. Azizah came with fresh fruit or anything she was allowed to bring to ease the pain of imprisonment for Reza and his cellmates. Mariam carried boxes of sweets and cookies to give Reza.

Mariam's long straight hair was pulled back from her face in a ponytail. With no make-up, she looked plain, somber, and her eyes glistened with tears. Ali noticed that every time she tried to talk, her grief seemed to choke her. There was always a long line of people waiting outside under the hot sun, wondering whether their loved ones were even in this prison or if they had been transferred to another location. Many parents were denied visiting permission. Outside the prison, mothers fainted in the blazing sun, fathers cried, daughters begged for mercy or for a bit of information about their loved ones.

§

Reza's incarceration was devastating for Azizah. After her husband had passed away, she had come to rely on Reza as her eldest son for almost everything. He became the new father figure, the man of the house, the guardian of the younger children; losing him to prison was unfair, absolutely unjust to Azizah. He was the most loyal son any mother could have hoped for. Distraught and scared, Azizah could not eat or sleep.

"He is a wonderful son," she told everybody, "doing everything he can for his family. How could the police arrest him? What kind of country is this where its youth are perishing in prison?" Azizah kept asking everyone— taxi drivers, grocers, neighbors, strangers in the street.

People just looked at her, lowering their eyes, uttering not a word, not even offering a sympathetic gesture. Those were terrible times, and Azizah was asking dangerous questions. Everybody knew the government would do anything to find out about those who opposed the Shah's rule. Nobody could be trusted, not even a poor woman who dared to openly criticize the government. She could easily be a secret agent, paid by the Savak. Looking away, people kept their opinions to themselves and their mouths shut, for they knew spies didn't come only in men's clothing.

But Azizah didn't care what the others thought; her eldest son, her one source of pride and relief, was in prison, and she couldn't take it alone. The fear of losing Reza was pushing her to the verge of madness. Azizah couldn't stay quiet as if nothing had happened; she could not bear her pain silently.

§

Mariam's only goal was to get Azizah in and out of the prison compound safely, to make sure that she wasn't going to snap at the guards and cause any trouble. They heard many horror stories shared by other parents, told again and again, each time with new details. Mariam tried to build an invisible wall to protect her mother against the prison's prying eyes and the suspicious guards.

Ali saw all of that, and could not get Mariam out of his mind. He sought her whenever he and Reza were called into the visiting room simultaneously. His eager, anxious eyes sought Mariam on the other side of the bars every visiting day, and did not rest until he located her, his heart jumping out of his chest. She glimpsed him watching her from the other side of the bars.

"Who is that man?" Mariam asked Azizah once when they left the visiting room, intrigued by his unrelenting attention. He watched her more keenly than the guards.

§

Ali's mother, Zahra, sitting on the other side of the bars, noticed her son's eyes drifting to the next window. She always gave a complete report about how the family was missing him, how many people she had contacted to obtain his release. She would tell officials that he was the most devoted son any mother could have. Zahra desperately needed Ali at home to take care of her family if they were not going to become homeless.

Zahra knew every line in Ali's face; she didn't need to study him closely to recognize the dark circles under his eyes. She could tell if he slept well or not, how much weight he had lost. Following Ali's eyes, her view landed on the somber young woman standing at a nearby window. Zahra could not help but ponder the tragedy of life. Ali had been in college for three years and had not mentioned a girl's name once, and, now in prison, he was in love. She watched his eyes drifting dreamily to the young woman standing next to her mother.

Zahra saw love unfolding in prison; she was a witness to the first glance, that initial pause, that moment when an innocent look lasts barely a second longer and turns into a thrilling sensation. Ali's mother saw this potent gaze; it said it all without revealing much. She didn't know whether she should be happy or heartbroken.

§

"Is your sister married?" Ali asked Reza one day after returning to their cell.

The two men read each other's mind clearly. They came up with a clever scheme—they asked their families to arrange their weekly visits on the same day, at the same time; that way, Ali and Mariam could see each

41

other through the bars. To be able to steal a look gave Ali lasting pleasure in those days and under those conditions. Exchanging glances with Mariam became more frequent, shy smiles were added, and the sweet taste of possibility invigorated Ali. He counted the days until his release, when he could finally marry Mariam. Ali had fallen in love without exchanging one word, without once holding Mariam's hand, without being able to freely walk down the street with her. They had not talked about their dreams and hopes, their ideas and ideals. The prison brought them together and kept them separate; he took their silent, longing glances as a sign of love. The further apart their visiting windows were on any given day, and the more obstructed their view, the more Ali felt the joyous pang of love.

Ali and Mariam started writing letters to each other. To escape the prison censor, they quoted classical poetry.

> I put up with the hardships of the sea
> No need for the sea, once I earned my pearly wage.
> No need to deal with false prophets because
> When friends are here, false claims disparage.

Pretending they were siblings, their letters escaped the scrutiny of the prison guards who screened all correspondence between inmates and the outside world.

§

For Ali, life was an ill-fated accident. He was not political or an activist; he had just happened to be in the wrong place at the wrong time, on the wrong side of the street with the wrong group of people.

"How many wrongs have to happen to change one's path forever?" Ali asked himself.

He was interested in politics, but not involved in any serious way; he simply couldn't afford to be political when his family needed him so badly, especially his mother. Of course imprisonment for any cause had never crossed Ali's mind.

"We have to move to Tehran," his mother had told Ali one day, unable to hold her tears back. "Nobody can find a cure for your father here."

She had spent so much money going from doctor to doctor. Everybody said something different, but no treatment worked. Zahra watched her husband turn into an invalid before her eyes. She sold everything they owned, borrowed money from relatives, and moved the entire family, only to have the same distressing experience. All the money was wasted on different useless treatments. Each doctor pursued a different remedy, none of which worked.

After fighting a mysterious illness for years, his father finally died when Ali was sixteen. This meant that Ali had to work one or two jobs from a young age. His father's pension was far from enough to support a family of six. All the children started working as soon as they could, doing whatever odd jobs there were—helping out the neighborhood carpenter or the grocer. His older sister quit school to find a job. Working at construction sites was Ali's first summer job during high school. He started teaching private math classes when he got accepted at the university. He was so bright that his teachers always recommended him for tutoring. The family was barely making ends meet; however, they were in Tehran, and that was the place to be—where everybody from small towns wanted to live in the '70s. The city offered many promises—wealth, money, and success—even to those who had recently arrived.

"Mother, I'll work two jobs. Hamideh is working too. Between us, we can make it," Ali consoled his mother. "Things will be better."

He had lost his father, but he hadn't lost hope. "We have each other. You've kept the family together all these years, doing people's laundry and cleaning houses. Now that we are older, we'll do this together. You don't have to work so hard anymore," Ali told his mother proudly.

They would carry on without their loving father, but the family was young and hopeful. Ali was bright and hardworking, and uncles and aunts were willing to help out here and there. Nothing could hold him back.

§

In his junior year, right before the beginning of the spring term, he received a letter from the university. Skimming it, he reached the line, "… You are not allowed to attend classes. Your student ID will not be validated until your tuition is paid in full."

Ali could not believe it. They were taking away his right to attend classes? How could that be? Yes, he hadn't been able to pay his full tuition, but he had promised to do it by the end of the term. He was no cheat; he just needed a few more months to save enough, or maybe borrow from his relatives again, like he had done last year. He stayed up most of the night, rehearsing different scenarios in his mind, talking to his professors, to the dean, even to the president of the college if necessary.

"This is a mistake," he told his mother. "A correctable oversight. I will ask for an extension. Will borrow some from Uncle Hadi. It will be all right," he promised Zahra and Hamideh, who were watching him nervously.

He had his speech ready about why he should be allowed to attend classes. Being an articulate speaker was one of his talents. He was born with it. His classmates always pushed him to be the spokesperson, the class representative. He had a beautiful baritone voice—even if people didn't understand his topic, they were taken by his voice. He walked to the school, determined to negotiate his way into his classes with a promise to pay his tuition in full by the end of the term.

Approaching the university block, he noticed a gathering of people. That area was always crowded because of all the bookstores. It was a fun place to saunter and check out new books. Block after block of bookstores, no end for the enthusiastic readers to find the latest European translations, contemporary literature, or classical Persian poetry. A place for intellectuals and the educated to see and to be seen. Passing the bookstores, he noticed familiar faces in the crowd, classmates he knew.

"What's up? What are you all doing here?" Ali asked with a concerned look; he had never seen so many students gathering outside the university gate like that.

"We've been expelled because we can't pay our tuition. We're not allowed to enter the university or to go to classes," a few said. "It's absolutely outrageous. Why shouldn't we go to class? Because we're poor?"

Ali knew most of the students; many were like him, simply unable to pay their tuition in full for the time being, but they'd pay it sooner or later, if allowed an extension. They were bright and dedicated, working in addition to going to school full-time; it was a heavy load, he knew well.

"We are demanding an extension. We want to go to class. If we miss classes, we'll fall behind," one of the students said angrily.

"We should talk to the dean and explain our situation. He'll understand," Ali said, trying to emphasize collaboration with the authorities instead of confrontation.

"The guards have blocked the entrance. We can't even enter the campus to explain our situation."

The crowd was getting bigger and louder, creating a false sense of power. Even those students who had paid their tuition were joining the group out of curiosity or sympathy. They didn't think it was fair to go to class while their classmates and friends were not allowed to enter the university compound.

Ali could understand his fellow students' frustration and anger, but he didn't want trouble. He remembered a few students who had disappeared overnight during the last couple of years; nobody knew their whereabouts. Nobody dared ask. Ali took note of the increasing number of students, but he didn't see the army trucks driving fast to the corner. He was struck by the number of poor but talented students, like himself, who simply wanted to be able to go to school.

Perhaps the biggest mistake he had ever made in his life, he thought to himself time and again, was crossing that street. If only he hadn't gone to the other side to see what was happening. If only he hadn't gone to school that day, he wouldn't have been picked up by the uniformed guards who poured out of the army trucks.

§

Looking back on his life, Ali realized the depth of the changes he had undergone. The passage of time had in a way silenced him. The optimism that he spread by his mere presence was gone, and his mesmerizing voice faltered every time he opened his mouth. Ali had lost his desire to speak, bitterly realizing there was no point in talking if nobody paid attention. Mariam never listened to him; perhaps she had her own monologues in her mind. Ali used the minimum number of words, only what was absolutely necessary. Over the years Mariam didn't complain about his growing silence.

If in the prison Ali was counting days to be released, he was now counting years to be freed from his marriage. His prison term was over, but his marriage was supposed to be forever, till death did them part. But, no, he was not going to accept this marital sentence forever. He would wait a couple more years, until his youngest son came of age and didn't need him or his mother as much. Jamshid was going to college next year and Hamid would finish high school in three years. The sound of his sons and their friends playing games made him smile; Ali took joy watching them play Monopoly and darts. He had tried to be the father he always wanted to have, the father he never had. They were balm for his tired soul. He had reached inner peace, and now he would wait for them to grow up. He knew he'd have custody if he divorced Mariam; that was the law of the country. No doubt about that, but for now they still needed their mother.

Ali wanted to be there for his sons, to give them all he could. He didn't want them to have to work as young as he had. Life was hard enough. He kept telling himself, I have endured prison, I can take a few more years of this.

§

At the end of his prison term, the first thing Ali did was to visit Reza, who had been freed some months before him. Walking to Reza's house, his step felt light, as if he were flying. He couldn't stop smiling to himself since he had left the prison. He noticed passersby looking at him and then taking a second look. He didn't know it was his smile.

Ali reflected on his incarceration. It was the thought of marrying Mariam that had given him hope. He was able to forgive anybody and anything; he even treated the prison guards respectfully, not holding them responsible for their crude behavior. Ali was ready to start a new life and he wanted to start with a light heart. Enough hardship, enough grief.

Reaching Reza's house, Ali waited for a few seconds to bring his heartbeat under control. Looking up and down the street, he noticed it looked deserted, no kids playing soccer with a plastic ball, no peddler screaming over a loudspeaker about his delicious melons or fresh bread. It was oddly quiet, nothing like it was supposed to be in the early evening hours.

All of a sudden Ali felt alarmed, as if eyes were watching him from behind closed curtains. He rang the doorbell, wishing somebody would open the door quickly, but nobody answered. He waited and pushed the doorbell harder, hearing the harsh ring clearly.

He stepped away from the door, cautiously walking to the kitchen window that was open just a little. The curtain moved faintly and he sensed a silent commotion behind the window. He knew he was being watched by more than one pair of eyes from the surrounding houses.

Hearing light footsteps, he walked back to the door, which was now opened slightly. It was Reza who had recognized Ali from behind the kitchen curtain and come to the door, gesturing for him to enter quickly. The family was gathered in the living room, looking distraught and exhausted. They hadn't looked this troubled even during their prison visits, Ali thought to himself. Shocked by the dreary greeting and teary eyes, he was embraced by Reza who held him tightly for a long time. Everybody was crying.

Ali had no reason to be sad; he wanted to embrace Reza happily, to congratulate Azizah for having her son back home safe and sound. He had come to ask for Mariam's hand.

Nobody thought of taking the box of sweets that he was holding awkwardly.

"My son is out of the prison, but they have taken my Mariam," Azizah sobbed uncontrollably.

A piercing pain mixed with panic stabbed at Ali's chest. He grabbed the nearest chair to sit.

Azizah had difficulty talking, speaking through her tears. "They have taken my daughter. Who knows what they're going to do to her?" she cried.

Listening to Azizah and Reza, he found out that Mariam had been picked up by the police and nobody knew her whereabouts. Ali moved closer to Azizah on the couch, holding her rough hands in his, but his thoughts were going in a hundred different directions.

"I could tell Mariam was up to something; she had started spending a lot of time away from home, never telling me where she was going." Azizah's eyes were bloodshot; a cup of tea and flat bread and cheese sitting in front of her were untouched.

"She was bringing all these papers home. I knew, but I kept thinking that with her brother in prison, she wouldn't do anything wrong. Oh, my sweet daughter. I wouldn't have taken her to the prison every Friday if I knew this would happen."

Apparently, visiting Reza in the prison had become a turning point for Mariam. Seeing distraught mothers and fathers in tears every week, and listening to dreadful stories, had opened her eyes to harsh political realities. Her admiration for Reza, her sympathy for Ali and other prisoners, had gotten her involved. Moved by the suffering of those in prison, and their sudden transformation into heroes in the eyes of their friends, Mariam could no longer remain the detached protector of her mother. She had become dedicated to a cause embraced by many young men and women determined to end the Shah's dictatorship. To them, anything would be better than the ruling dynasty.

Like hundreds of her generation, Mariam had joined an underground group and decided it was time to risk everything, if that was the price to free the country, to liberate the innocent perishing in prisons, to end poverty and imperialism.

Ali sat there listening to Azizah talk feverishly. Heaviness seized his chest. All the euphoria he had felt walking there had left his body, his mind, his soul. He was more tired than ever before.

§

Ali was devastated and felt scared of what might happen to Mariam. But he was also proud of her. Not many women are willing to rise against a dictatorship and risk their life, he thought to himself. It takes a lot of courage and determination. She was not like other women, wearing miniskirts, coloring their hair, and wearing bright make-up. He was convinced that Mariam wanted to do something for people who were denied their basic civil rights. For people like him and Reza. And that demanded admiration.

Yes, he was scared for Mariam, and troubled about what they might do to her in prison, but his love grew stronger, his dedication more intense. He'd wait for her no matter how long it might take, and write letters like she did for him. A Hafez poem he knew by heart came to mind.

> He added then, "That friend they hanged
> > High on the looming gallows tree—
> His sin was that he spoke of things
> > Which should be pondered secretly,
> The page of truth his heart enclosed
> > Was annotated publicly.

> But if the Holy Ghost once more
> > Should lend his aid to us we'd see
> Others perform what Jesus did—
> > Since in his heartsick anguish he
> Was unaware that God was there
> > And called His name out ceaselessly."

Ali had a plan; he would visit Mariam in prison, pretending to be her brother, perhaps using Reza's ID, and tell her that he wanted to marry her.

But his plan did not work out exactly the way he wanted.

The two families were swept up by what was happening in the country. There were frequent demonstrations and strikes in the late '70s, and the opposition had gained momentum. Men and women, young and old, anybody who was suspected of the slightest unpatriotic sentiments, was arrested. If earlier Ali and Reza met as cellmates and became friends, now it was Mariam and Ali's mother who ended up in the same prison at the same time. The secret police had started picking up more women, showing no double standard. While previously it was thought that women were weak-minded and content with their conditions, it didn't take long for the regime to discover that women were as capable of taking steps against the monarchy.

It was a time of massive imprisonment of both the apolitical and the activists, a time when even uttering a critical word against the Shah's regime could be devastating. Everybody was rumored to be a secret agent, a government informer. Ali's mother and Mariam were imprisoned, but for entirely different reasons.

§

Like Ali, Zahra was apolitical. But their little home was near the prison, and her kitchen window opening to the street was always left ajar. Zahra heard countless crying mothers and fathers on their way to prison. Without thinking, she opened her door to the distraught parents or wives who were worried about their children and husbands. Time and again she saw desperate people sitting under a shady tree on the sidewalk by her house where a stream watered the trees. She overheard them, men crushed by worry, incapable of soothing their grieving wives or mothers. Women weeping uncontrollably because they didn't know if they could see their son, brother, or husband the next time they went for a visit. Zahra, suffering her own pain of having Ali incarcerated for unreasonable accusations, opened her heart and her door to these grieving families. Before long, people started ringing her doorbell when they came for a family visit at the prison. It was only a matter of time before the secret police found out that many people entered and left her small home, and much information about the prisoners got exchanged at the small rickety wooden table in the kitchen.

Zahra was taken to prison for investigation.

Although the authorities soon realized that this poor woman did not belong to any underground guerrilla movement and was not a major threat to the nation's security, she was given a year and a half prison sentence. Upon her release, she was instructed not to offer hot tea or cool sherbet to grieving people whose unpatriotic children had betrayed their government, their Shah. True patriotism meant letting people faint from thirst under the blazing sun and not offering hot tea on cold winter days.

§

It was Zahra who asked for Mariam's hand in prison on behalf of her son. Ali thought that under the circumstances that was the most beautiful gesture, especially given the fact that he had no idea when Mariam might be released. No prison could crush his love; no dictator could take hope away from him.

He recited poetry day and night, taking solace in the veiled messages carried over the centuries.

> With your long curled eyelashes
> You brought me a thousand doubts
> When your sleepy eye flashes
> A thousand pains in me come out.
>
> O thou, companion of my heart
> Memories of friends my mind depart
> There is not a day that from the start
> Your memory I do not tout.

The world is baseless and old
Lovers shout out and scold
Magic spells take their hold,
This is love's sorrowful route.

Separation sets me on fire
My circumstances are dire
May the nightly breeze inspire
With a whiff of what it's all about.

As he wrote letters and Sufi poems to Mariam, Ali imagined listening to Mariam reading them aloud, although he had never heard her voice. They had exchanged only momentary glances. Only longing gazes. Only short letters written in ink. And ink has its own enemies—air, water, time. It has an evaporating quality, just like love.

§

Everyone saw Ali and Mariam as a perfect match. Azizah worried no one would ever marry Mariam, her reputation stained by prison experience. Zahra was equally concerned about Ali not being able to find a wife; he didn't have any money, and his prison record would hamper his work opportunities. Furthermore, he would have to hide his background from any woman he was going to marry. No one would agree to marry a political prisoner.

Ali was overjoyed to think that his marriage proposal might make the prison experience easier for Mariam in the same way her presence across the bars in the prison's visiting room had made his. Daydreaming about her gave him hope. Counting days and planning became his obsession.

Her suffering and her bravery ignited a selfless love in Ali. The more he thought about Mariam, the more dedicated he became, admiring her courage and self-sacrifice.

§

Ali surveyed the living room and kitchen, surprised to see that everything looked as it did two months ago. As if time had stopped. Mariam had not purchased new furniture in his absence. She usually managed to buy new things every time he left for his trips—a new coffee table or sofa, lace curtains, another set of china. He could never tell what would be added the next time he returned. Mariam had a never-ending urge to buy something, and she wasn't alone. Most of their friends were busy buying things, as if ten years of war and shortages had created an insatiable desire to accumulate.

When Saddam had pressed the war into the cities, bombing Tehran in the dark of night and the middle of the day, it had a devastating psychological impact. The war was no longer limited to the southern parts of the country. Nobody knew which neighborhood would be targeted, whether their house was going to be the next one to collapse in the raid, taking the entire family with it in the middle of the night, or only the women and children and elderly, if the bombing happened in the daytime. When the sirens stopped, people automatically felt relieved, only too conscious of the fact that while they were unharmed this time, some other family had been devastated. The feeling of relief came with an immense sense of guilt.

Many were thinking, "Thank goodness we're alive." Cautiously leaving their basements, their next move was to rush to the phone, calling parents, sisters and brothers, uncles and aunts, friends and co-workers.

The war was too close to ignore. The survivors' guilt and fear were debilitating.

During the war, many had instinctively become recyclers. War conditions and economic embargo had created a strong sense of frugality because nobody knew what would be available or scarce the next day—diapers, coffee, meat, cleansers. Most everything was subsidized by the state, but that didn't help much. People stood in lines, often not knowing what they were standing for. If there was a line, they stopped. Even though they might not need whatever it was, they could always sell it later on the black market or give it away to friends and relatives.

After the war, stores gradually filled with new goods, and people could not stop shopping. Nobody threw old things away for fear of scarcity again; they just kept everything while purchasing more stuff. Who knew when this prosperity would be ended by another economic embargo? Another war? Sanctions had eased, and yet the frenzied yearning to buy and to accumulate had become a way of life.

§

Ali first noticed the change in Mariam when new little things started to appear in their house—a ceramic sugar bowl, perhaps a plain tea set. He welcomed these additions, taking them as a sign of recovery, a renewed interest in life. Mariam had even started experimenting with new recipes.

This was the same woman who had believed entertaining family and friends was a waste of time. After she had been freed from prison, Mariam was dedicated to canvassing poor neighborhoods, educating the masses about reasons for their poverty, and teaching them how to change their situation. She had come home late regularly and sometimes disappeared for a few days. It was only a matter of time before Ali found out that Mariam had been continuing her covert activities after her release. Marriage, Ali found out only later, was a façade to hide her subversive political activities.

"As long as the poor don't have enough to eat," Mariam said accusingly, "bread and cheese is a luxury for us." Ali started cooking for both of them, for Zahra when she came for infrequent visits, and for the few relatives who stopped by now and then. Mariam couldn't bother with such petit bourgeois luxuries.

And that was only the beginning. Ali was getting to know a Mariam he hadn't known before. The new Mariam, or was it the real Mariam, was nothing like the girl he had imagined. For her, all of life's necessities had a distorted meaning—cooking was a waste of time, entertaining friends a bourgeois extravagance, nice clothes a sign of vanity, visiting family, especially Ali's relatives, meaningless.

The marriage that everybody was so happy about was crumbling from within. Mariam's political teachings demanded blind obedience to an ideology that denounced ordinary happenings, everyday relationships. Expressing happiness was tantamount to denying suffering in the world, owning more than two pairs of pants extravagant. Coloring one's hair was viewed as a sign of westernization. Shoes with holes became the right kind of possession, a sign of dedication and commitment. Strictness and a life of austerity were demanded for a good society, and Mariam and her comrades were eager to obey, never hesitating to correct non-believers, accusing them of materialism and bourgeois sentiments.

§

The eventual overthrow of the Shah's regime only intensified Mariam's political devotion. When a short period of openness was followed by the new government's efforts to establish its power, Mariam and her comrades found renewed reasons to fight. They saw religious rule by the mullahs to be as bad as secular dictatorship. Mariam's brief absences turned into longer disappearances. Azizah had lost any say over how Mariam conducted her life. Ali's mother saw her son struggling to hold his family together, doing all the shopping and cooking; she noticed that Mariam was rarely home, but she kept quiet. Mother and son prayed silently, hoping that Mariam would not disappear completely. They all knew that they could lose her to the same old prison under the new government that saw religion as the only path to salvation.

In the early 1980s young people were trying out their voices in an open political realm for the first time, believing they could bring constructive change in how their country was run. And like the previous regime, the new government did not discriminate in its punishing ways; nobody was immune if suspected of disloyalty. The new regime saw women quite capable of dissidence and subversive activities.

Mariam's blind devotion to a leftist political ideology had made Ali's life unbearable. When Mariam insisted on material asceticism, all Ali could think was, What kind of luxury did I ever enjoy in my life?

In some respects, Ali did respect Mariam's ideals, but he believed that no positive transformation would come out of such hollow ideologies. He watched many youths turn their backs on their families, on life, unaware of the grave consequences awaiting them. He knew it would be only a matter of time before the new regime would lash out against opposition groups. He had the ominous suspicion that thousands would lose their lives—not to mention the agony and suffering they would cause their worried families.

But who could take away hope from idealists, from dreamers, from youth?

§

"We have a family to take care of. Your family and mine," Ali said again and again. He fought Mariam's stubborn political conformity. "This is a volatile situation; we have to act rationally." But Ali's words fell on deaf ears. Ali felt absolutely worn out, disillusioned about life, politics. About personal or even romantic relationships. Reflecting on his life, he realized how immature he had been to marry her. He had mistakenly assumed that their shared prison would make them a good couple. That longing glances meant love.

So when new things started to show up in their house, he saw them as a psychological break from the past, if not, a revolutionary (so to speak) transformation. He looked forward to new objects appearing in their home. He thought they presented a readiness to embrace life in a new capacity, to enjoy simple things. Ali even encouraged Mariam to shop, to buy anything she fancied.

Welcoming the change in their immediate surroundings, in drinking tea in matching china cups, Ali started to envision a second life, a new possibility for happiness in their intolerable and unhappy marriage. Maybe they could heal their shattered spirits, their broken hearts, their wrecked relationship.

§

Stepping into the bedroom, Ali suddenly noticed a grand new bed. He stopped right at the door, his eyes widening, as if he couldn't believe what was in front of him. Mariam quietly walked into the bedroom, a placid expression covering her face, and went straight to the chest of drawers, taking out a shirt and underpants for him.

"I've rearranged everything," she said nonchalantly. "Your shirts are in the third and fourth drawers."

Ali's shocked expression revealed neither satisfaction nor displeasure. Having learned to keep his feelings and thoughts to himself, he had become a man of few words.

The bed looked spectacular, almost like a fancy sailboat, nothing like the folding metal cot he had used for the last sixty days. It was huge, with elaborate wood panels and a beige leather headboard. The bedspread was a striking floral with elaborate crème and burgundy peonies mixed with deep orange roses. He was taken by the rich colors; they were so different from the desert and the drab tent that had been his private space.

He got a glimpse of Hamid and Jamshid in the hallway, tiptoeing, curious to see his reaction. Looking at Mariam, Ali found her eyes exploring his, waiting for him to say something.

"Where have you found such a grand bed?" was all he managed to say. The days when their eyes did the talking were long over. "It's so huge!" he added, trying hard to keep the rush of sarcasm and spiteful comment to himself.

He wanted to say, when was the last time we embraced, the last time we were intimate? What did we need a new bed for? A bed this size? To ensure enough distance between our bodies? But he didn't.

The new bed spoke of intimacy, sweet talks, pleasurable embraces, physical closeness, but for Ali, it was only a big lie. He saw the bed as an empty symbol of a life that never existed between them. If a sudden movement might have brought an unexpected embrace in their earlier days, this bed made sure they remained in their own universe, with an invisible wall encircling each body.

In a way, he felt that all his married friends were living a lie. King-size beds were new additions in every house; the women showed them off. Friends and sisters praised it while the men looked at each other in bafflement without uttering a word. The bed was a luxury item, but the reality was that wives insisted on sleeping in the children's bedroom or in the extra single bed. Rarely did husbands and wives find each other simultaneously on the same grand bed.

Ali couldn't think of a single friend who was happily married. Questioning his generation's idealism, he thought to himself—we were envisioning a new era. How naïve of us! We wanted to change the world, and now we are miserably stuck in our own relationships, failing wretchedly in making even a happy marriage, a happy family, let alone building a new country.

§

From a life of severe austerity, owning only one pair of worn shoes with holes in them, Mariam had gradually begun to desire affluence, as if she wanted to compensate for years of self-imposed deprivation. What started as a trickle turned into a flood. The woman who had insisted on educating the masses came to the realization that she had been missing out on life. Every time she thought about those young women who lost their lives to quick executions, she couldn't hold her tears back. But she also heard about those comrades who managed to escape the country, living a life of freedom in the West. As she struggled to save her country, her people, she saw herself fighting against not only political dictatorship but cultural tyranny as well. She felt abandoned by her male comrades; all those who did not see forced veiling as a cause to fight against. All those who advocated equality but were ready to pack and leave if the situation became too dangerous, leaving the young and vulnerable behind.

Mariam was disillusioned.

It was time to rethink, to reevaluate. She saw a new generation of women who were demanding elaborate weddings, gold jewelry, exorbitant dowries. She had asked for no dowry; that was against her principles. But times had changed; Mariam dreamed about being a real woman, one who was taken care of and provided for.

§

What happened to Mariam? Ali wondered bitterly. What happened to all those ideas about changing the world and creating a new culture? Was all that an impossible dream? A product of youthful imagination? As though more clothes, bigger beds, gold jewelry led to happiness. Ali turned these thoughts over in his mind, examined them, reviewed them, to no avail. He counted his blessings that his family had survived the most difficult times, especially through Mariam's long period of what he derisively called her revolutionary stage. He remembered the cold sweat covering his body the day he discovered the cyanide pill in her purse. Now she had reversed her course and embarked on another revolution—rampant consumerism, and he was expected to provide for it.

Crushed by life, that's how Ali felt. By the times he was born into, by the marriage he had chosen, by Mariam's early extremism, and now by her desire to live an extravagant life.

Looking back at his generation, he thought of friends who had lost their lives to the revolution. Those who survived were forced to abandon their hopes, condemned to a monotonous, despairing existence. They carried the unbearable weight of loss—loss of hope. Many lived empty marriages held together by pity or shame of separation.

Ali wondered about the shallowness of youthful thinking. Weighing his present against his past, he concluded, right or wrong, that his generation critiqued the rampant luxury of the rich because their own poverty was too painful, but now they were trying to live just like the wealthy.

§

Ali was an engineer, a practical thinker. He had married Mariam and he was now planning his separation, thinking about having his own small apartment. He would divide everything equally with Mariam in spite of what the law dictated; he'd be fair in his divorce. As an intellectual, he believed in equality between men and women. It was true that Mariam worked part-time only after the kids started school, but she had taken care of them. He would even let her stay in their house and keep all the furniture. He didn't need much. He had enough clothing to last him for a lifetime, and he would be happy with a few dishes, a small bed, no pretenses, and yes, of course, his books, which had been banished to the basement since they moved to their new home. Who needed five sets of teacups made in China? One cup was enough for him, just one. He would buy another if this one broke. He would take music lessons.

A faint but purposeful smile appeared on Ali's lips. He could finally picture himself doing what he had always wanted—living a simple life, reading books, and playing the hammer dulcimer, the heavenly instrument of his childhood dreams. It wasn't too late; freedom was only a couple years away. His sons could stay with Mariam if they so chose. He'd pay for their college tuition, for their weddings. Nice weddings, the kind he never had because he had no father to cover his expenses. How many times over the years he had wished his father could see how he had provided for his mother and his siblings from an early age. Ali wanted to tell his father: See, this is what I have done. I have a nice home in a respectable neighborhood. Come in, see the yard. Look at the rose bushes. Your picture is always on the wall, in the living room. I haven't forgotten you.

Although completing his engineering degree took much longer because of his prison term, he nevertheless graduated. Ali couldn't stop thinking about his father the day he received his diploma and certificate. Tears filled his eyes. Everybody thought they were tears of joy. But they were tears of having no father to share this momentous life experience with; he was the first in his entire family to graduate from college.

The day he got his first mining project, Zahra told him, "Your father would be proud of you."

§

Getting out of the shower, breathing calmly, Ali wrapped a towel around his body. He wasn't ready to put on his clothes. The warm shower had calmed him; he could still feel the rhythm of the bus, but the fatigue of the trip had left his body and now he felt light. An unconscious smile spread over his face.

He let his body sink in the cushiony chair in the bedroom. Where did this chair come from? The bed was so grand that he had completely missed the chair and its ottoman. A new chair with a raised back, ideal to rest his head. The chair engulfed him in its plush cushions, enticing him to forget his work, the mining site, the world and its problems.

There was much commotion in the kitchen, pots and pans clanging against each other.

"Hamid, why don't you pour tea for your father?" Ali heard Mariam say.

"He's still in the shower."

"No. He's done. The water pressure is back. Jamshid, the cookies are in the cabinet. Put a few on a plate."

The new chair was too comfortable to move. Ali contemplated putting his feet up on the ottoman, something he normally would not do; it was pure luxury.

Quietly pushing the door open with his foot, Hamid brought in freshly brewed tea, carefully placing the tray on the small end table by the chair. Jamshid followed him, carrying the plate of sweets, biting into a delicious cookie. He kept the plate to himself, out of his brother's reach. That was always his favorite game.

Watching Hamid tenderly, it suddenly dawned on Ali that he had spent most of the bus ride plotting to turn his sons into fatherless boys. No, he couldn't do that to them; nor could he subject Mariam to the same suffering his mother had endured, living without a husband, without a man in the house, everybody pitying her and her children—his sons. Zahra had to do everything on her own, saving every penny. Ali could give everything they had to Mariam, but how could she support herself in old age with a part-time job that offered no security? How could she pay for the utilities, house repair, her health or car insurance? What would she do when a repairman came to fix the television or the kitchen plumbing?

Pretend to still be married? What would the neighbors and shop owners think about her? Everybody would see her as easy prey.

What about his future daughters-in-law? They wouldn't respect Mariam, knowing that Ali had divorced her; nothing would stop their gossip.

Ali felt sorry for Mariam, recognizing that she wasn't happy in their marriage either. He could start all over, find a young wife, start a new family, but there was no way Mariam could marry again or live on her own income. Nobody would marry a divorced woman of her age. Fifty. Forget it. She wouldn't have a chance up against all the young pretty girls who were more than willing to marry older men as long as the men had money. No, he couldn't bring himself to cause humiliation for a woman he had tried to save years earlier, for a woman who had given him hope in the most vulnerable stage of his life. He couldn't humiliate the mother of his children. He was not that selfish.

§

Everybody was gathered in the bedroom, Ali on the new chair, Jamshid and Hamid lounging on the bed as though it were theirs, and Mariam on the floor, comfortably leaning against the bed.

The boys were telling the story of how the deliverymen brought the bed to the second floor. It was a seamless and hilarious account, Jamshid starting each sentence and Hamid finishing it in his deep baritone, and Mariam laughing freely, clearly enjoying her sons. Their excitement was contagious, as though they had rehearsed the story numerous times for his sake.

Drinking his tea, Ali realized his sons had grown into young men; he loved Hamid's deep voice and Jamshid entertaining sense of humor. It was as if he could turn every little incident into a comical story. That's what they all needed.

Taking in the scene, the four of them would, from the outside, appear to be an ideal image of family. Such an appearance would, of course, ignore the numerous holes and gaps, disillusionments and dissatisfactions as perhaps all appearances do. Ali was living the life he'd chosen, and he could end his life-sentence any time. Any day.

The Paris of the Middle East

1977

AN AVALANCHE OF accusatory words swept the quiet room before the door was fully open.

"*You* did it! *We* didn't want this. Remember? You have always done what *you* wanted. It's never about me, my dreams, what I might want in this damned life." Pausing for a second, Nader threw a despising look at his wife. "This is your baby. You hear me? You wanted it—you take care of it. I want no part of it."

Turning on his heel to leave, Nader bumped into the nurse who had rushed to the room. Jumping back reflexively, she knocked over the other nurses who were running in behind her, craning their necks to see what was happening. He was momentarily taken aback to see a group of nurses gathering by the door, staring at him.

Alarmed by the noise, somebody yelled, "There's a fight."

But there was no fight. Nader hadn't even fully entered the room to divulge his profound anger at the birth of his first child. He had stood right by the door as if going inside the hospital room would have been an acceptance of fatherhood.

The two women in the room had remained quiet during the verbal attack, offering no words of reconciliation, appeasement, or anger. Their wordless response had made Nader only more livid, as if he were talking to deaf people. He could not adequately express his deep-seated fury. After Nader left, Mahta felt too exhausted to say a word; she just looked at her mother Pouran, unable to hide her embarrassment. Pouran had moved to the center of the room, holding onto the bed's railing, trying to shield her daughter from the violent words fired at her.

Covering Mahta with the blanket, Pouran kissed her on the forehead and whispered, "Don't worry, dear. Men are like that. He'll come around. Just give him some time. He is still young." But she knew well that her own husband had had two children by the time he was twenty-eight, providing for his growing family like a responsible man should.

Mahta closed her eyes while holding onto her mother's hand with one hand, and wiping away silent tears with the other.

Everything had happened so fast that the nurses didn't get a chance to avert their eyes, nor did they move aside quickly enough to make room for Nader to leave. They had seen all kinds of sentiments expressed at the births of babies, but never such a spiteful outburst. Fathers came with beautiful presents, boxes of sweet, colorful flowers—whatever they could afford—to congratulate their wives. But not Nader.

"He is a handsome man," one nurse had whispered to the others. "What's wrong with him?"

In a few minutes, everybody on the floor knew what had happened. It didn't take long for the nurses on other floors to hear the story, with various embellishments. Nurses stopped to see Mahta. Some came out of sympathy, others out of curiosity. A few entered the room with the pretense of offering sweets, a present from another happy family, to take a good look. Others discreetly peeked into the room, shaking their heads in disbelief. By evening, Mahta and her mother felt like they had been surveyed by every nurse in the hospital. Room 44 had become the center of interest, gossip, and sympathy. They were served dinner twice, with extra ice cream.

Mahta and Pouran could hear the whispering nurses behind the door all day. Some had happily concluded that their own husbands were not bad men after all.

"Yes, he is a handsome man, very good looking, but you should have heard what he told his poor wife," one nurse told the others. "My husband never speaks like that. He loves our two daughters."

1972

Nader picked up Reza and they drove to their usual meeting place. He loved driving in the early morning hours. There were hardly any cars on the streets, with only street sweepers hard at work. He often wondered how the crew could see what they were sweeping in the dark. The entire town seemed to be still dozing, not ready to face the day. No shops were open except for the bakeries; the aroma of freshly baked bread wafted through the street. Upon reaching the gravel road, Nader slowed down to park the car as close as he could to the running stream. He had the whole alley to himself except for a few parked cars belonging to other hikers. In a couple of hours, there wouldn't be any space left for parking.

"What a rowdy group of students; they don't stop arguing even at such a wicked time of day," he thought to himself as he heard his friends engaged in a loud discussion. If Fine Arts students frequented discos and ice-skating rinks for fun, engineering, law students, and social science students went mountain climbing. The hiking trips were a regular event, and with the lengthening of daytime and the approaching summer, Nader and his friends started at an earlier time every week.

The early morning hours gave him an immediate chill as he got out of the car. Moving quickly, the two friends walked up quietly to the boisterous group standing next to a hot-beet seller's stall. The steam rising from the stall was the only source of heat. The aroma of the dark, baked beets was appetizing.

Scanning the group, Nader could see not all of the hikers had arrived.

"You didn't bring Cyrus?" Amir cried out when he saw Nader.

Cyrus was the newest member of the group, and the one who was late for everything. He and Nader had bonded very quickly. To stop him from being late, Nader had come up with the clever idea of picking him up every time, but the night before Cyrus had called to let him know he'd get there himself.

"He's late again? What's his excuse this time?" The group sounded like a youth choir, echoing each other. They were annoyed, but in a lighthearted way. Nobody really wanted to badmouth Cyrus.

"Oh, he probably worked late last night," Mino chimed in.

"Cyrus has not worked a day in his life. He parties all the time, and tells us he's very busy," said Amir who didn't appreciate all the breaks Cyrus got from his friends. "He thinks his time is more precious than ours."

"He doesn't realize our beds are as warm as his," Elli said. She often made such remarks for their pure shock value.

"We don't have to wait for him. He can catch up with us," Amir suggested.

"Cyrus called me last night and said he'll be here," Nader said.

Cyrus was a sweet, charming guy. Most everybody appreciated his company. He was bright, knowledgeable, and could turn the simplest event into the funniest story. People always wondered how he came up with such hilarious stories.

"Let's give him a few minutes and we'll take off if he doesn't show up." Nobody ever questioned Nader's calls.

Nader knew his friends were not going to wait for Cyrus long, but the long walk to the top of the mountain wouldn't be the same without him. To give Cyrus time, Nader lunged into talking about the book he had finished the night before.

"I finished *The Stranger* last night. I couldn't put it down."

Mino asked, "What is it about?"

"Well, this is the plot. The protagonist Meursault hears about his mother's death, and he's not even upset, as if it's no big deal to lose his mother." Pausing for a second, he added, "I felt both repulsed and intrigued. I couldn't get it out of my head, dreaming about it the whole night. I can't tell if I was dreaming about Meursault or what. Everything seemed so eerie and yet very real. Perhaps I was dreaming in absolute consciousness."

"Yeah, we read it in my French class last semester at Alliance Francaise," Elli said. "Meursault's mother dies and he feels no grief. How could that be? He kills an Arab because he's having heatstroke. I mean he really kills a man, and he has no feelings of remorse."

"Meursault perceives life as meaningless," Nader said. "As if life is worth nothing…"

"Well, as far as I'm concerned," Elli interrupted, "if you are not saddened by your own mother's death, life has got to be meaningless for you."

"Meaninglessness becomes meaningful for him only in the context of death," Nader contended. "Meursault thinks he has no free choice—like most of us. Are you free to live the way you want?"

"What do you mean he is not free? He shows no love for his mother and no sadness at her funeral. He goes and kills a man! He plots to have a woman who is suspected of infidelity beaten up. These are not free choices? He makes all these decisions by himself as a free man," Elli answered passionately.

The discussion was getting heated between Nader and Elli. Others were listening intently. They hadn't read the book, but since existentialism was the latest fad among the intellectuals, many college students were eager to hear more about the story. Elli, whose grandmother was French, was like an encyclopedia of French culture and literature, always ahead of the rest of the group and trying to encourage them to read more European literature.

"Some of us are able to make decisions about our life, but most of us have no freedom. We are given one life, and we have to live it without ever questioning the rules that chain us," Nader started again. "You want to tell me I am free to do as I please? Freedom is a luxury only people in the West enjoy."

Mino, who had remained quiet until then, tried to relate the discussion to her personal experiences. "Perhaps what the story implies is that everybody has a choice—even in our countries. Like I can decide whether to marry the suitor who was visiting last night."

"Are you going to marry him?" Elli asked.

"Well, if I do, I must wear a scarf every time his mother or his relatives come over for a visit. I left the living room and didn't go back. That was my choice, and nobody can take that away from me."

"If you don't marry him, you'll never find a husband," Amir said teasingly.

Everybody burst out laughing.

Listening intently to their conversation, the beet seller looked quite puzzled. He threw an appraising look at Mino and said, "I'll marry her anytime. I can go to her father's house this evening and ask for her hand."

A moment of embarrassed shock descended on the group. Staring down at the beet seller, Mino felt speechless, with her mouth left open in disgust. Nader immediately came to her help by saying, "God Bless you, old man, but our friend is ..."

Nader's voice was muffled by the sharp sound of a car braking, and a joyous honking farther down the alley. Looking toward the car in the alley, they saw Cyrus jump out of the car and sprint toward them, his hair still wet, a big smile brightening his face.

"Sorry, sorry, I hope I am not late. You should have gone without me. I am not late, am I? You can't imagine what happened! It's so good to see you all. Let's go. What are we waiting for? Everybody is here, aren't they?"

As Cyrus was greeting everybody excitedly, Nader noticed another figure slowly emerging out of the parked car, patiently making sure all the doors were locked. Wearing large fashionable sunglasses, she calmly walked over to the group. A distant but courteous smile on her lips was the only clearly visible part of her face. As she reached the group, she acknowledged them by gently removing her sunglasses. She waited quietly for Cyrus to introduce her.

"Oh, everybody this is Mahta, my baby sister. I told her how wonderful you all are!" Cyrus exclaimed. His joy and sincere smile were contagious; nobody gave him a hard time for being late.

The group finally started hiking up the dirt path that would lead to the mountain cap fifty minutes late.

§

The mountain provided no shelter, except for sporadic coffee houses located along the river. After climbing, the hikers rested on carpeted benches along creeks, surrounded by trees, a small oasis. They put their tired feet in the freezing cold water that still carried patches of ice from the snow-covered Alborz mountain range.

Nader and his friends saw themselves as a peerless bunch. They aced the most challenging university exams. With a voracious appetite for books, they read whatever they could get their hands on, spending hours rummaging in bookstores to find the latest translations of European writers. They were reading Sartre and Fanon, Aime Cesaire, and Dostoyevsky. Weekly installments of Simone de Beauvoir were published in literary magazines. They frequented traditional teahouses—places where a generation earlier no woman ever entered. They enjoyed sitting on wooden benches, watching old men watching them, sometime hearing their spiteful comments about the younger generation. They also went to modern coffee shops and restaurants. The novel opportunity to navigate their world in mixed groups, and the mere presence of women in such places, had an invigorating impact on them. They were tasting the exhilarating feeling of freedom that nobody before them in Iran had experienced on such a grand basis.

They were keenly aware of being the first generation to go to college on en masse and coeducationally; they had a different life to live. Coming from modest and religious families, some tried to desexualize women by claiming to have platonic friendships, an exotic term they had newly learned. They called the women sisters, while unsisterly waves of attraction continuously assailed their hearts, keeping them awake at nights and anxious during the day.

§

Nader envisioned living in Paris, having coffee at Les Deut Magots and dinner at Café de Flore, walking down Boulevard Saint Germaine and Rue St. Benoit. He knew the names of many Parisian streets and boulevards, and he was able to tell friends and relatives where to visit if in Paris. Elli showered the group with additional information gained through her grandmother and traveling abroad. Reading the *Second Sex*, she had become an expert on Simone de Beauvoir.

"Did you know Simone de Beauvoir and Jean Paul Sartre live together? They have never married. Both of them have had other lovers, too."

There was always a moment of awkward silence after Elli's announcements.

"Elli knows about the most outrageous things!" Amir said out loud.

The group often needed a few moments—perhaps hours or even lifetimes—to digest what Elli would say.

Glancing mischievously at the guys in the group, Elli continued, "Simone de Beauvoir has a lover who is much younger than her. And he is not her only one." The women just listened, trying to avoid eye contact.

"Well, they are intellectuals—whatever that means," Amir said. "Living in a different country. Inheriting a different culture. We are not like them."

"Who said we aren't?" Elli countered, sounding annoyed by Amir's blind acceptance of difference as an explanation.

§

Nader asked his mother Fati whether she loved his father when they married.

"An irrelevant question," she responded. "We married. We raised good children. We took care of our parents in their old age. I nursed your grandmother for two years when she was bedridden. Your father never married a second wife, insulting me like your uncle did with his family. He provided for his family. What else do you want?"

But for Nader, the question was more than relevant. Inasmuch as his parents' lives represented a successful family story, for him it was the model to avoid. He saw himself, his generation, as the force to bring change in centuries-old traditions such as arranged marriages that required total obedience of the wives, and created rule-thirsty husbands and distant fathers who were more a source of fear than love—like his own father. No, the time for a cultural transformation had arrived, and he envisioned a life totally different from that of his parents.

Nader's father, Mr. Moradi, had married the girl his mother had chosen for him. And his own mother married the young man her parents had picked for her.

"Why did you marry father at such a young age?" Nader asked Fati. "You were only fourteen."

"Yes, I was only fourteen, but sweetheart, I am from a different generation. Born in 1920." Fati shook her head as if her youngest son was incapable of understanding such simple things in life. She had actually welcomed the handpicked suitors; they were a source of pride for girls her age.

"Everybody married like that. All my friends looked forward to marrying. We were just wishing our husbands would be handsome men. Marriage is too important a decision to be left to a fourteen-year-old with no real life experience."

A big smile appeared on Fati's lips. Her face beamed every time she recalled that first time when she got a glimpse of her future husband, Nader's father.

"There was a big latticed window in the living room, and one of the tiny colorful glass panes had broken and was never replaced. My little aunt and I peeked through that missing piece. Your father was a handsome man, just like you. Tall, wearing his military uniform, walking proudly into the room. Sitting like a true gentleman, like a Russian prince. He knew I was watching him because he kept looking around, searching for the source of whispers and mirth, but he couldn't see us. We were giggling hysterically in the other room, admiring his elegant uniform and his polished shoes. New and shiny. Finally, he figured we must be somewhere behind the latticed window. He at last turned ninety degrees to face our direction, as though he could actually see us. I guess he had decided that now that he couldn't see us, he would at least give us the opportunity to have a good look at him. I felt I was having a silent conversation with him through that missing glass. That was it—those silent conversations. That was enough for me."

Every time Fati told that story, she relayed it with such joy, talking like a fourteen year-old, as if it were the mid 1930s again. However, that was the only story she ever told her sons. It seemed like her lifelong marriage was encapsulated in that moment, the groom sitting like a prince and Fati hidden behind a latticed window.

What she never shared with her sons was the reason behind her parents' hasty decision to find a suitable husband for her. That she was an ambitious student in her small school, dreaming about becoming a doctor. There were midwives and women healers who relied on folk medicine and herbal treatment, but hardly any Western-trained women doctors. As rumors of the forced unveiling of women spread like wildfire, many parents panicked.

"Sending our daughters to the streets unveiled?" Fati's grandmother had asked fearfully. "That's absolutely unacceptable."

Fati remembered hours of heated but hushed discussions between her mother, grandmother, and father. Her father had no problem sending his daughters to school unveiled, but the grandmother was adamantly opposed to such impropriety. That was contrary to everything she was raised to believe in. She had threatened to move to Mashhad if they sent Fati to school unveiled. Fati's father had obliged because he didn't wish to disrespect his mother, the family matriarch.

The end of schooling meant early marriages for many girls. When unveiling became the law of the country in the 1930s, young daughters were kept at home. Many women imprisoned themselves in the confines of their homes and courtyard rather than venturing outside unveiled. For Fati's grandmother, remaining veiled and secluded was more honorable than losing respect in the eyes of the family and the community.

Fati did not challenge her parents—she filed away her dream of becoming a doctor and obediently accepted to marry the man she saw as her "Russian Prince," the groom her parents agreed was the best in a long line of suitors. While Fati spoke about her dream of becoming a doctor to her daughters, she never revealed anything to her sons.

"In my generation, you didn't question your parents," she repeatedly told her three sons and two daughters.

Fati became a wife at fourteen, and Mr. Moradi found himself married to a girl his parents had chosen for him.

All he did was to ask his mother to find a beautiful and fair skinned wife for him. Mr. Moradi's mother had obliged; Fati was indeed a very light skinned girl.

That was so archaic, Nader thought to himself, to be forced to marry at such a young age. Somehow the fact that his father also didn't have much of a choice in the matter escaped his attention. Somehow he was not cognizant of the fact that his father had obediently listened to his parents too, never questioning the wisdom of their choice for his life.

I am not going to marry like that, Nader thought. No. I am never going to marry, period, was his final decision. The fact that all his sisters and brothers had arranged marriages did not cross his mind. He was the youngest son, his mother's favorite, and he was in charge of his life, a life free from constraints.

§

Who felt the first pang of affection, of desire? Which one couldn't wait till the next hike? Whose eyes lingered a moment longer, hypnotizing the other? Was it at the mountain coffee house? The dare over who could keep their feet longer in the creek? The rare view of uncovered toes immersed in the ice-cold water? Was it an unexpected, stolen glance at Mahta's polished toes, painted Chinese-lacquer-red?

Going from feet to feet, Nader and his friends told hilarious stories about each other's toes, cleverly psychoanalyzing each other on the basis of their toes' form and length. They burst into uncontrollable laughter.

Was it that Friday morning, July 17, when Mahta kept slipping during the hike? She was wearing a new pair of sneakers. The clerk at the shoe shop had sworn on his mother's life that they were perfect for mountain climbing.

"So much for trusting a shoe salesman," she said after an hour of trying to stay on her feet. Her sneakers had no grip. After several slips, she finally said, "I am going back. There is no way I can handle the high slopes with these sneakers."

Moving in an orderly line, the entire group stopped.

"No, we can all go back if you need to return," Mino volunteered.

"You've barely started. Not fair. You all go ahead without me," Mahta said.

"We can't let you go back on your own. It's dangerous," Amir objected.

Cyrus interjected, "It's all right. I'll go back with Mahta."

But Nader, the most experienced hiker, said, "I'll stay with Mahta. You guys go ahead; we'll wait for you at the first coffee house on your return."

Everybody felt relieved that they could go on. The group picked up speed, while Nader and Mahta started their downhill walk at a slow pace. They stayed close together because Nader wanted to be able to catch Mahta in case she fell. They were arm in arm after the first sudden slip, and it was okay because they had the perfect reason—slippery sneakers.

Nobody questioned the closeness, the budding intimacy that day and the Fridays that followed. In fact, nobody wondered about all sorts of friendships developing amongst the young hikers. All of their relationships were imbued with novelty.

Nader found himself at Mahta's side at all times, during the hike up the mountain and at the coffee houses. Mountain climbing expanded into the group seeking each other's company at poetry readings, art exhibitions, and in uptown restaurants with exotic names like Casablanca, Chattanooga, and Latin Quarter. In their hearts and minds, they were traversing Western cities without ever leaving Tehran city limits.

Walking side-by-side and sitting next to each other at restaurants brought the inching closeness of their bodies. An unintended touch, a gentle pat on the shoulder, a protective gesture crossing the street, were all ecstasy. The warmth of their bodies, the fortuitous contact of their hands left them excited and energized. Each casual touch carried a weight beyond their imagination. Nothing mattered anymore except planning the next visit to supposedly talk about, say, the new art gallery opening.

Longing to see more of each other, Mahta started visiting Nader at his house where he lived with his mother. Happy to have a throng of young people at her home, Fati was surprised to see Mahta staying after everybody left, or visiting alone. She noticed how Mahta gradually brought personal belongings. When Nader and Mahta finally moved to the vacant second floor, she remained quiet. For Fati, her son was beyond doing anything wrong.

The decision to live together without a formal marriage was indeed an incredible move for 1973 Tehran. Nader felt that their desire to live freely was strong enough to shatter what he perceived as meaningless tradition. Feeling victorious, he was at last breaking away, fracturing the seal of cultural taboos that guaranteed lasting, but loveless, marriages filled with unvoiced longings and unfulfilled desires.

§

Mahta and Nader experienced a glimpse of a life different from the lives their parents had led.

"This is 1973," Nader thought to himself, "a time to break away, to live freely." He was not like Meursault, Camus' anti-hero, who saw no hope in life. He decided he was not going to let either meaninglessness or tradition dictate his life's chances. Life became meaningful, and he was intent on enjoying every second of it.

Sitting at Café Naderi with Mahta and Cyrus, enjoying their café glace and chocolate éclair, Nader made a confessional statement. "We are path breakers, the trendsetters." His eyes seeking Mahta's, he continued, "Thank goodness we don't have to oppose the French rule, as they do in Algeria, or to fight a war, as in Vietnam or Pakistan. We just need to fight our own traditions."

Cyrus nodded his head in approval. Mahta couldn't agree more.

1977

Elli and her mother, Mrs. Valayat, turned their house into a sanctuary for their friends after Mr. Valayat passed away. People came and left as they pleased. Her father's early death was painfully sad, but they were able to start over. The two women had created a beautiful symbiosis, resembling two friends more than a mother and daughter.

Mrs. Valayat was often home, but she left Nader and Elli alone, retreating to the back rooms when he visited.

"I miss our gatherings!" said Nader.

"What happened to us, to our hiking group, to our exploring the city, having Turkish coffee right here at this table? To reading Sartre and talking Dostoyevsky?"

Elli quietly stood up to make coffee.

"I loved her. I really did," Nader said inaudibly, as if he were talking to himself. "But I never wanted to marry. Didn't want a baby. I thought we both wanted to be free. I was so happy when we moved in with my mother, living on the second floor. We had made a nice life for ourselves." He looked up from the table, seeking Elli's eyes, perhaps her affirmation.

"What did your mother think about you two living together without marrying?" Elli asked.

"Oh, she was fine with it. She loves me; I am her youngest son."

"Well, yes, I know that you're her sweet boy, but your mother is a religious woman. Didn't she think what you were doing was wrong?"

"Nah. You don't know my mother. For her, whatever I do is blessed. She never thought our living together was sinful, if that's what you mean."

Smiling to himself, he added musingly, "You see, my mother is an extremely open woman. She was happy for me to live with Mahta. Who knows, perhaps that's what she would have liked to do herself."

"Don't kid yourself. Your mother is a true believer. She may accept it for you because she realizes times are changing, but she would have never accepted that option for herself or for your sisters."

The aroma of the Turkish coffee filled the kitchen.

"Your coffee is always the best. It's so aromatic."

"I buy it from the Armenian store in Naderi Street, but Mom adds her own spices, especially cardamom, and it makes a world of difference." Without pausing, Elli asked, "So why did you marry Mahta if you were happy with the arrangements?"

"It wasn't my mother, it wasn't me," Nader paused, lost in his thoughts.

Reflecting back, he started talking slowly, "Mahta started acting differently. She no longer wanted to live at our house. She'd stop by for a quick lunch and leave right after, looking upset. I knew something was wrong."

"What was it?" Elli inquired.

"Cyrus finally told me. He was hanging out with us all the time. We had even set up a bed for him in our house. He was staying with us more than with his own parents. He loved the way we were living together, as a family but completely free."

Elli remembered how all their friends and families were astonished at the speed with which Nader and Mahta were breaking cultural norms.

"No wedding and they are living together? In his mother's house?" Many whispered while others said it loud enough for everyone to hear.

Nader and Mahta paid no heed for what relatives, shopkeepers, or neighbors said. If everybody condemned them, their small circle of friends regarded them as heroes, viewing them with awe. Friends' admiration made them more daring. However, while friends saw them as trailblazers, others perceived them as sinful hedonists to avoid.

Nader cherished their lifestyle, the freedom it offered with no binding obligation. No rule of law, no tradition. No signature to chain them together.

Elli probed him further. "What did Cyrus tell you?"

"He told me everything—how his parents were pressuring Mahta to either marry or end our relationship. That they felt I was taking advantage of their daughter. That I had no intention of ever marrying her. They felt disgraced; their family honor ruined by my actions. My actions!"

"Well, were they wrong? Did you intend to marry Mahta?" Elli asked.

Nader fell silent, "I guess not." Rubbing his forehead forcefully with the palm of his right hand, he tried to sort out his thoughts. He finally said, "But Mahta knew it; the fact that I didn't want to marry was nothing new to her."

"You can't blame her for what you finally decided to do. You agreed to marry her. You could have easily walked away and stayed free." Elli now sounded critical.

"But I loved her! I'm not a cheat or a swindle. I didn't intend to disgrace her or her family. I just wanted to live freely. Is that too much to ask for in this country? Why can't we live like normal people in other countries?" Nader countered.

"The problem is you think you're living in Paris," Elli said in a low tone. "This might be the Paris of the Middle East, but we are still in Iran. Remember your mother and her mother and their great grandmothers lived a veiled life. You want to jump a century in one generation?"

§

Nader and Mahta had married with no big ceremony. No white gown, no fancy black suit for Nader. No bouquet of little roses to be held in

Mahta's beautifully manicured hands painted with light-pink polish. Only a small gathering of friends. No elders were invited—a sin that wouldn't be forgiven for years to come. No honeymoon. Only a few presents from close family and friends. No pictures to mark the day. Mahta bought a yellow and white gold ring for Nader.

The wedding brought a fragile sense of normalcy to their life in the eyes of the family, neighbors and shopkeepers. Self-designated moral guardians stopped asking pointed questions. Instead new commentaries started.

"See, that's what they should have done a long time ago," many said. "What's this nonsense about living together without marriage? No respectable girl does that. Nobody will marry her when he dumps her for a young virgin."

The tide had settled, but the ensuing calm was the beginning of a tumultuous period for Nader—their marriage marked the end of his dreams to live as a free man, uninhibited by cultural expectations. The death of his dreams ushered in a new understanding of the power of tradition, and of the authority of the elders.

Mahta was now a wife, a newly married woman. Marriage had its own rules; it was time to build a new house with high walls to protect its sanctity, locked from inside and out.

§

The doorbell started ringing furiously. Opening the door in a state of alarm, Elli cried out, "What's wrong? Has anything ...?"

"I went to the hospital this morning," Nader blurted out.

Stepping away, Elli made room for him to enter. The good-looking, always properly-attired man, who everybody admired, didn't look like himself. Elli heard the uncontrollable anger in his loud but trembling voice. All their friends had kept quiet about Nader's behavior during the last few months when he found out Mahta was having a baby. Elli had advised him to think rationally, to act properly to avoid any future regrets. Only last week, she had told him in no uncertain terms that he was acting selfishly, that he should go back to his family, to Mahta, especially now that her baby was due any day. Now that the baby was born, she found him at her door in a frantic state.

"Come on in. I was just making tea. Did you see the baby?" Elli wasn't exactly sure what to do. She considered changing to a more proper outfit before making tea; she felt awkward in her relaxed housedress. Nader sat at the kitchen table; on the same chair he had spent hours ruminating the last few months. He didn't seem to notice what Elli was wearing. Elli poured boiling water into the teapot, letting it simmer.

"I didn't see the baby. I didn't even go to the nursery. Oh Elli, I said some horrible things. I don't know what came over me. I just wanted Mahta to know what she has done to me. Once and for all. For the record. She has ruined my life, my dreams. I had to tell her." Nader put his big, fine-shaped hands over his face, covering his eyes.

"Elli, her mother was there, too," Nader said solemnly.

§

Like a fugitive, Nader had escaped his own home, turning into a stranger in his own hometown. Unable to focus, he passed his days absorbed in a never-ending monologue. He had forbidden his mother from seeing Mahta, but Fati had secretly visited Mahta and her granddaughter at the hospital, promising to bring Nader back to his family. Everybody was waiting, but days turned into weeks and weeks changed into months of estrangement.

Fati never mentioned Mahta and the baby Helen. Nader's youngest sister, Azar, the one he felt closest to, did not mention Mahta's name either, but every now and then he heard hushed conversations: "Oh, she is so cute; her cheeks are just like Grandma's. Do you remember how well defined Grandma's cheeks were? She was a beauty even in her old age," Nader's older sister Mehri said.

"You should see her toes. Her middle toe is the shortest, just like Dad's. Somebody finally inherited that toe. She won't be able to wear sandals in summer when she grows up. Everybody will notice her short toe."

"Who knows, maybe by that time she can have a little plastic surgery and lengthen her toe? If her nose goes after Mahta's mother, she'll need a nose job too," Azar chimed in humorously.

Nader never asked who they were talking about, but he knew about his daughter's cheeks, nose, and toes even before he had ever set eyes on her.

Of all his friends, the only one he could freely talk to was Elli. His married friends acted as if they didn't know what was happening. Their gatherings had become infrequent and stifled, filled with awkward silences. It felt as though his actions were tearing apart the entire group.

Elli listened and asked questions, encouraging Nader to open up. He called Elli his psychoanalyst, desperately needing her to end the non-stop monologue in his head.

§

More than once Nader found himself driving slowly down his street. More than once he parked his car in the adjacent alley, wandering through the neighborhood, and finally walking toward his house. He was all ears by the time he reached the open kitchen window—that was the place where the women congregated in late afternoons. He was hungry to see or hear something. Anything.

Surveying his street and checking his house had become his new routine. He chatted with the store owners, and the dry cleaner who was his age. Everybody congratulated him on the birth of his first baby girl, wishing him a larger family, a son for sure. One Saturday afternoon he found himself in the dim, cool hallway, having no recollection of how his feet had walked him toward the door into his house. Had he opened the door or was the door left open? He couldn't remember reaching for his key to open the door. Once inside, he had no idea what to do next. He couldn't turn back and leave like a burglar. He could hear Mahta and her sister Ellahe in the living room, chatting. Taking a quick look at the balcony, he saw Pouran's maid hanging the laundry. There was noise in the kitchen, a voice, asking if everybody was ready for Turkish coffee. It was Armine, Mahta's best friend, who was always in charge of afternoon coffee.

Sensing the presence of another person in the house, a shadow in motion, hushed footsteps in the hallway, Pouran felt alarmed. Only she and Mahta had the key to the house. Everybody else used the doorbell. Opening the kitchen door quietly, Pouran quickly turned on the light switch, illuminating the dark hallway by the sharp stream of light from the crystal chandelier—a generous gift for the birth of her first grandchild. She had always detested that dark hallway.

Pouran had imagined a moment like this numerous times, rephrasing her first sentences over and over, trying to think of a composed reaction once Nader showed up. But with the passage of months, she had almost given up on that idea, thinking about the future of her daughter, raising a girl on her own in a country where the presence of a father was crucial in how a child was treated. The last thing on her mind was being confronted with Nader's image in the hallway mirror. His back to her, his face transfixed in the mirror, shocked by the light pouring down. It was as if there were two Naders.

Pouran hadn't spent a night at her own home since Helen was born. Nader knew Pouran would be there, but he was still stunned to see her. For a second, the thought of running away occurred to him.

"I should have rung the door bell," were the first words he muttered.

"This is your house. You're not a guest here. We are the guests here, not you!" Pouran replied sharply. But Nader felt like an intruder, a stranger walking in on people he didn't know, disturbing their quiet afternoon. He knew Mahta's friends and sisters were helping out. He had spied on them carrying heavy bags of grocery, heard them through the kitchen window chattering as if they were living there, but still, he felt paralyzed.

"Mahta is in the living room, nursing the baby," Pouran said quietly after a moment of silence. In spite of repeated rehearsal, that was all she could say, trying her best to control the avalanche of recriminating thoughts. She had felt physically attacked by Nader at the hospital. Her sense of self-respect was badly bruised; it was the kind of bruise that would leave a permanent mark. Pouran had suffered humiliation in front of the nurses, people she did not know. Having to lie to friends and relatives about Nader's whereabouts in the hospital, and afterward when they came to the house to visit, had shamed her deeply.

"On a trip? At a time like this? He should be here with his wife and baby. This is no time for traveling," people said in astonishment—or with malice.

Pouran had never felt so disgraced in the eyes of her family, friends, and neighbors.

§

Mahta and Ellahe were chatting away when she noticed Ellahe's sudden silence. Following her eyes toward the door, she saw Nader.

Months of waiting had finally come to an end. Nader was standing at the threshold of the living room, motionless, wordless, not taking a step back or forward. Just like an intruder.

Looking shocked, Ellahe stood up, "Where did you come from?"

This was the greeting, the moment they had all imagined and rehearsed endlessly. All the women had prepared for this moment, wondering on their own, and collectively, about how they should react when Nader finally showed up.

Waiting for a few moments in the kitchen to calm her beating heart and angry mind, Pouran calmly walked to the living room. She had decided long ago that if Nader came back, it was best to properly greet him in spite of all the anger she harbored in her heart. As if she had not witnessed the scene at the hospital with her own eyes, shielding her daughter against Nader's violent words and rude manners. As if she had not deserted her own husband and other children for months to take care of Mahta and her baby.

"Some things are better left in the past," she had told herself repeatedly.

§

Much commotion descended on the previously tranquil house, with the women trying to politely but quickly leave the couple alone. All the basic necessities they had gradually brought over during the last six months were scattered around in different rooms. However, before a timely and collective departure, Pouran quietly walked to Mahta, who was still sitting on the couch, took the baby from her, and pensively walked up to Nader.

Kissing the baby on her forehead, she stared at Nader, who was trying to avoid direct eye contact.

"This is your daughter. You should be proud of her. She will be your life-long companion and friend." Her voice trembling, tears welling up in her eyes, she continued by saying, "All the love you give her will return to you. With girls, even if you don't love them, they will love you forever. Even on your deathbed. Enjoy this gift of life, take care of her. And don't throw it away because of some vague ideals."

Thrusting the baby into his arms, Pouran quickly turned to leave, afraid her emotions might spill over. She was scared to say something she'd regret later. Nader held the baby awkwardly in his arms.

Stealing a quick look, Pouran sensed a feeling of silent remorse in Nader, perhaps a flash of shame and regret. Wishful thinking, she thought to herself as she left the house.

§

The women left and the house went absolutely silent. Nader had returned but he did not remove the curtain of silence he had drawn between Mahta and himself. He was back, but his deep discontent kept him aloof.

Mahta spent the night in the nursery. The first night she slept alone in her house without the help of the women who had gathered around her to compensate for the missing and obstinate husband. Without her mother bringing a warm bottle of formula and taking the baby to her bed, Mahta felt lonely.

Nader was now the husband, the man of the house, but he felt defeated by Mahta and her baby, by the army of the women who supported her. For Nader, Mahta's desires had a coercive force, buttressed by the power of tradition.

It had not occurred to him that no one would question a married woman's desire to have children after five years of marriage. He never thought it was his responsibility to provide for his wife and newborn baby. Examining his dreams of escape had never occurred to him.

For Nader, Mahta marched armed with the power of culture, kin, and custom. Her motherhood unveiled her invisible power while exposing his failure; fatherhood signified the end of his dreams.

1982

"Honey, your dad will help you with your science project," Mahta told Helen tenderly, knowing only too well that Helen had been waiting for Nader the entire afternoon.

"But he's not back, Mom," Helen responded sulkily. "Tonight is his bridge party. Did you tell him before he left?"

"Yes, I did. I also called him a half-hour ago. He promised to be back by 8:00. He'll be home soon." Mahta crossed her fingers as she made another promise on behalf of Nader.

Helen could easily finish the project on her own, but she loved to work with Nader. Those science projects were the one activity that brought them together.

The distant father became a patient teacher while working with Helen. The more complicated the homework, the more absorbed the daughter and father became. Nader explained everything clearly, much better than her teacher. Those were the rare times when the father and daughter sat next to each other at the dinner table, Helen's books neatly organized on the left, her sharpened pencils and clean erasers at the center.

They were a good team, working ceaselessly. Helen enjoyed sitting by her dad, smelling his cologne mixed with the sweat of the day. She loved his long, well-shaped fingers moving smoothly over the pad of paper. His fingernails always looked polished, unlike her chemistry teacher, who had dirt under his. Nader watched Helen carefully, her hand moving hastily on the paper, solving complicated math puzzles with no difficulty. He was amazed at the speed at which she learned, her concentration, thinking he was never as quick as she was at her age. She absorbed everything the first time he mentioned it. No need for repeating the same thing twice. She was a math whiz; formulas came to her easily.

Their studying hours were the most joyful time they spent together, with Mahta being all eyes and ears in the background. Helen giggled happily as she finished problem after problem, proud of herself, pleased to make her father smile. Hovering around in a silent and invisible way,

Mahta brought them delicious snacks and cookies to keep them together a bit longer, fading into the background instantly, as if the cookies had materialized on their own.

Nader felt so relaxed after each homework session that they often sat together and laughed over nonsensical stuff, with Helen telling stories about her eccentric teachers, how nasty Mr. Amin or Mrs. Bahar were. She liked Mr. Mani, her geography teacher, though.

"Mr. Mani has a baby. He showed us her picture. She is so cute! He calls everybody, 'My sweet daughter.'" She paused for a moment. "Mr. Mani's eyes are green. I mean really green. He has a dimple on his chin, too. But he is always a little unshaven."

The girls could tell on which days Mr. Mani had shaved the night before or in the morning before school. Nader laughed heartily; he couldn't believe that girls Helen's age paid so much attention to such details.

"So, I'd better shave properly when your friends come over."

"Dad, all my friends think you're the best. Even my best friend's mother, Mrs. Saif, has said so."

"Better than Mr. Mani?" Nader inquired.

"Even better than Mr. Mani."

Obviously, his premature gray hair had not reduced his appeal for Helen's friends, Nader thought to himself contentedly.

"If you like your geography teacher so much," Nader threw the question at Helen once, "would you marry him?"

"Dad! He's already married." Pouting her lips, Helen put her pens and erasers in order. "Mrs. Mani is a little chubby, though; she drives to school every Monday and Wednesday. Their baby is always in the child seat, and they switch places. He drives them home."

"No, that's not what I mean. What if he wasn't married? Somebody like him with really green eyes and a nice dimple?"

Helen went quiet for a long moment, longer than Nader expected. Pondering the question, she finally came up with an answer that sounded only too familiar to Nader.

"No. I don't want to marry. Never."

Taken aback, Nader's eyes sought Mahta's, but he only detected her moving shadow in the hallway mirror.

§

When Helen graduated from college, Mahta threw a big party for her. The graduating class was invited to celebrate the official beginning of their adult life and the end of four formidable years of college. They were exchanging information about jobs, who was planning on going abroad to which country, and who was getting married.

Nader was trying to help out, putting flowers in vases, greeting the guests at the door, and leading the men to the living room. The women were directed to a side room to change before joining the party, for they came properly attired in their long outer garments and head-scarves as required by the country's law. It would take them a good while to emerge like the latest fashion models, flashing their bare skin and showing their beautiful curves. Long, flowing hair adorned their faces, complementing their every move. Their bodies covered in black was like a distant memory. Only a couple of women still kept their head-scarves.

Overwhelmed with flower bouquets, Nader grumbled, "We're running out of vases. I don't know what to do with the next bouquet."

"Just mix them up," Mahta said absentmindedly. She was busy putting stuffed grape leaves in a big round dish. Pouran had been cooking for the past two days, making dishes specifically chosen by Helen. They had talked about the menu endlessly, for days and nights. Everything on the table was from Helen's wish list.

"Dear, this feels almost like a wedding," Pouran whispered to Mahta, who was standing close enough to hear what her mother said. The two exchanged a meaningful glance.

The family was prepared for a big party but not for the stream of people who kept coming. Everybody had brought a friend or two, a junior classmate, a brother or sister. The house was overflowing with people. One corner of the hallway was covered with presents of all sizes. Helen and her friends were the guests of honor. They were the center of the party, hugging and kissing, sharing survival stories about endless studying for this test or that project. Their joyous laughter filled the entire house.

The family stayed in the kitchen and the back rooms and did not mingle much with the guests, but every now and then a group would go to the kitchen to greet Mahta and Pouran, thanking them for the delicious food and staying a few minutes to chat. Nader found himself standing by the door, drawn to the guests, and listening to their lively conversations. He noticed that Helen was clearly the center of the party.

Nader heard Helen's name in every story told and retold. She was summoned to group after group, never able to remain with one longer than a few minutes. The more he watched her, the more he felt a strong sense of pride, realizing that she was clearly admired by her friends. Inching closer to the living room, he found himself moving among groups. Helen's friends were inviting him to join them, politely addressing him, inquiring about his opinion about the job market, his college experience, the economic embargo and its impact on the country. All were listening to him with a sense of admiration.

§

"That was a wonderful party. Thank you, Dad. Thank you, Mom. Thank you, dearest Pouran," Helen said joyfully. The women were lounging around the kitchen table, too tired to clean up the party mess. It was time for gossip. Pouran took her shoes off to let the kitchen tiles cool her tired feet. Mahta had changed to a more comfortable garb. Helen was still in her fancy party dress, too excited to change.

Nader retreated to his study on the second floor where he had put a single bed years ago. He was wondering how the women still had enough energy to chat. His feet were hurting, his body exhausted, and he felt a tornado was raging in his mind, mercilessly throwing his thoughts into so many corners. Trying to focus, he opened his bookcase, and reached up for his collection of Khayyam's verses, hoping to calm his disquieting thoughts. He knew Helen was using his library, adding her own books to his collection. He always knew what she was reading because she left a colorful paper whenever she took a book. His study became her sanctuary during the day. She acted as if she didn't hear Mahta calling her five times from the first floor, finally giving up because she didn't want to climb up fifteen steps.

Sitting down on his comfortable big chair, clutching the book in his hands, he leaned back staring at his bookcase. He had started buying books again, hopeful to find time to read them instead of busying himself with evening news after work.

"Will I ever be able to read all these books?" His logic told him, "No, never." Not content with this response, he reasoned with himself, "Helen will be reading them. I don't even have to tell her what to read; she reads on her own."

A slight but bitter smile covered his face, a pang of regret filling his heart. Nader had come to admire Helen. He knew she preferred his company to her mother's; Helen consulted him regarding every important decision she had ever made in her life, and yet, he had remained the distant father. There was something he could not forgive; something he could not let go.

He could not love his own daughter completely without a sense of resentment, for Helen came between him and his dreams. He could not love Mahta, for she signified the death of his aspirations, and the beginning of his mourning for the life he had not been not allowed to live.

§

A loud thump shook him out of his stupor. The book had dropped to the floor. Picking it up, he tried to close his eyes against the rush of thoughts and emotions interweaving, colliding, demanding explanations, condemning. A dream or a nightmare?

Quiet footsteps in the hallway were followed by a few hushed taps on the door. Remaining motionless in his chair, Nader firmly clutched the book in his arms. A sign of self-protection? He always psychoanalyzed himself.

A couple more soft taps, and the footsteps retreated after a few moments. Familiar with the sound of her footsteps, Nader knew it was Mahta who had come upstairs to his study to check on him. She never stepped into the room when he was there; she had the room cleaned by the maid, but she never bothered him in his sanctuary.

§

The first party was for Helen and her friends, and the second one for the family and friends, a big gathering but with much less noise and excitement. Mahta and her mother were greeting the guests, bringing endless cups of tea, offering sweets, and putting plates packed with layers of fruits in front of the guests.

Standing in a corner with Elli, away from the others, Nader was looking at the family scene as though he were watching a foreign movie with no subtitles.

"Elli, I am so proud of Helen." Catching Elli's inquisitive look, he added, "I am. Really. Don't look at me like that! I admire her, her intelligence, the determination she exhibits, her popularity with her friends. She has barely finished her degree and she has a job offer. Nothing can hold her back."

"And …?" asked Elli.

A long pregnant pause. "I don't know," Nader finally said, despairingly. "I feel like I'm not her father."

"What do you mean you feel like you're not her father? Do you want a DNA test to find out if she is your daughter?" Elli said. "Look at her. She is your daughter more than she is her mother's. Her arched eyebrows. She has your father's toes, the short toe. And all that you admire in her, her intelligence, popularity with friends, her math genes, her dogged determination, all come from you. She is your Xerox copy, in full color. And you say you don't feel like you're her father? What more evidence do you want?"

There were times Elli showed sensitivity, and times she brutally confronted Nader with the reality he adamantly refused to accept. There were times Elli embraced new ideas—her life was the embodiment of a new vision. She had refused to marry, turning down many proposals. Coming from a wealthy background, she was economically independent, and she taught private French language classes. And yet there were times she genuinely questioned the choices she had made. She found much in common with Nader—they were both dreamers, fancying a life that was perhaps possible only on other continents, for people speaking a different language, inheriting a different history. As a woman, Elli had personally paid the price for her dreams; remaining single had proven to be challenging. At her age, she had started thinking about what if she had her own children, a girl like Helen. What if she had a husband who would take care of everyday things, who would drive her to the doctor's office, who would hold her at nights when she woke up worried about aging as a lonely woman. Elli felt the heavy burden of loneliness.

Sensing the anguish Elli felt, Nader quietly said, "I know, we feel we have failed. Our dreams changed into fanciful ideas. Look at Mahta. She is a strong and practical woman; she knew dreamers fall behind in this world."

Nader's eyes followed Mahta across the room. "Look at her. She is still beautiful."

It seemed like Mahta's success had come at the cost of blocking Nader's desire to build his own house of ideas. Nader found himself weak in the face of Mahta's strength, in her drive to succeed in spite of all the obstacles she faced.

Lost in his thoughts, Nader continued, "We were thrown into a whirlpool of impossible dreams. There was a short time for questioning and rebellion, and there has been a lifetime for submission."

Elli was feeling uncomfortable standing in a corner with Nader longer than it was acceptable at family gatherings. Their relationship had always invited long stares and hushed comments, but Nader was oblivious to his surroundings as usual, not minding the turning heads and inquiring glances. Eyes moved from Nader to Elli to Mahta. Those eyes had never stopped wondering.

Gingerly approaching them, Helen brought two big cups of freshly brewed tea. Taking advantage of the subtle interruption, Elli embraced Helen, putting her hand on her shoulder. "Your dad can't stop talking about how proud he is of you."

A little surprised by Elli's quick move, Nader patted Helen on the shoulder and said, "Your grandmother was right when you were born. She knew you'd make all of us proud."

Cuddling up to Nader, Helen murmured, "Dad, you know I couldn't do this without you. We've done it together. Do you remember all those math and science projects we did late into the night?"

Gently pulling himself away, Nader held Helen at a distance while keeping her hand in his, "You're a gem, Helen. Any father would be proud of a daughter like you."

Piano Lessons

PARVIZ WAS CONTENT taking the long way home. He preferred to leave the car for Sara and walk most days. It was quarter to six, and he would have liked to kill a little time before getting home, but he couldn't think of anything to do.

The sweet spring air felt fresh; most people had left town for the New Year's holiday and the impact was quite visible. The air was cleaner, the traffic more sane, the noise of the city less jarring. Holding his coat on his arm while he walked, he was breaking a mild sweat. He liked strolling, taking a few steps on one sidewalk only to cross over to the opposite side of the street by the next block. The blossoming trees and bushes were captivating this time of the year. He could get a glimpse of the spring flowers blossoming above the top of the tall walls surrounding the yards. Ornamental iron gates allowed the passersby to get a fuller view of the gardens. He enjoyed the scent of jasmine wafting from house number 176, the climbing rose bushes in house 186, and the lush wisterias two blocks down. The possibility to steal even a quick glance of people's yards, at the beauty hidden behind the walled gardens, brought a happy smile to his face.

"Have you noticed that the young tiny leaves are pistachio color?" he had once asked Sara excitedly, pleased to have come up with an exotic name for the color of the new growth on the forsythia bush in their own yard after its yellow flowers had faded.

"Why, you mean *green*?" Sara said as she walked by the bush, indifferent to its showy branches meandering left and right, as far as they could.

"Well, yes, but they are pistachio now. In a few weeks, they'll turn solid green." Seeking Sara's eyes, he continued, "They'll be deep olive by the end of summer."

"We should have them trimmed. They are becoming monstrous," Sara said, turning to go back into the building.

"No, not at all," he almost screamed, appalled by her violent suggestion. "They won't flower next year if we trim them in the fall." He couldn't believe Sara showed no interest in their garden. She didn't even like houseplants, let alone outdoor bushes and perennials that lusciously came back year after year, demanding little work and admiration.

"I am not a homemaker," she told him awhile after they married. "I am a chemist. I take no pleasure in housekeeping, in cooking, cleaning, or gardening. That's not me."

§

In the early seventies Parviz didn't know what he was looking for in a wife when he fell in love with Sara. He noticed her the first year she entered the university. Although he was a sophomore, he didn't dare talk to her. It was not appropriate for serious male students to strike up friendships with women. Engineering students were mostly from the provinces and came from traditional families. Parviz was no exception. He just watched Sara from a distance, and, finally in his senior year, faced with the prospect of never seeing her again, he decided to write her an

108

introductory letter. He awkwardly handed the letter to her sealed in a plain white envelope one early morning after exchanging pleasantries. Hoping nobody saw him, he tried his best to look as inconspicuous as possible. At the end of the short letter, he had made a formally worded marriage proposal.

Sara didn't write back, for it was not deemed proper for a woman to write to a man. But the next time she saw him, she cordially acknowledged him without mentioning anything in particular. Parviz had already proposed in his letter, but he didn't think he could directly speak to Sara about marriage. Instead, he asked his older sister, Mansoureh, to act as an intermediary.

"What do you like about her?" Mansoureh asked him.

"Ah, I don't know."

"Well, you want to marry her, don't you? Have you taken her out for lunch or invited her to a movie? There is a Clint Eastwood movie."

"No, of course not."

"Then how do you know she's the right person for you if you haven't spent any time with her?"

His pause was so long that Mansoureh thought he hadn't heard her question.

"Well, that's how mother and father married."

"That was a generation ago. And in Tabriz. Remember, we are living in Tehran now. Boys and girls date and get to know each other before marriage."

"Not in the chemistry or engineering departments. We don't date our classmates." Parviz said confidently.

"But how do you know she's the right girl for you?"

Looking at the white wall, he shrugged his shoulder, "Maybe it's her eyes." He didn't want to say anything about her height.

"So, it's just her eyes?" Mansoureh sounded puzzled. "You mean a girl's looks is the only thing that's important to you?"

"Well, naturally if it were only her looks, there are other pretty girls," said Parviz, trying to sound calm and rational. Pausing for a few seconds, he added that she is also very bright, hoping that would be the end of their conversation. Noticing Mansoureh's inquisitive look, he added reluctantly, "I just know she's the right girl for me."

Sara was from Tehran, born and raised there. She was one of very few girls studying engineering. Parviz had noticed that she got the highest grades even in the most challenging courses. The toughest professors seemed to like Sara, always looking at her when asking a trick question, as though they expected her to be the first to speak. He could tell other students were attracted to her, too. Somehow, her intelligence was captivating.

And of course, her looks. She was tall for a girl and pretty in a unique way. Her dark green eyes drew attention. Parviz tried to take some of the same classes Sara did, sitting quietly in the back, taking pleasure in looking at her flowing, soft, light-brown hair. Watching her every move and gesture, he had silently fallen in love. But Sara appeared oblivious to the romantic overtures of men, the charming way they addressed her, the polite way they held the door for her.

§

Sara had scores of friends. At least in the beginning, Parviz hadn't given it a second thought. She would usually spend her evenings on the phone, chatting away with friends, her mother or relatives. Recently,

Mina, their daughter, was spending more time with her friends, too. Parviz didn't agree with Mina's excessive partying during college, but he refrained from directly voicing his opposition. He had never understood his daughter, and, deep in his heart, he was happy to have only one child. Sara completely supported Mina's every whim, disagreeing with Parviz every step of the way. Sara had virtually raised Mina on her own, paying for her piano and dance classes, skipping work to chauffeur her from the time Mina was only five years old.

Recently, Sara had bought a brand new car for Mina. Now, Mina didn't even have to wait for a ride, or ask for permission to use their car for an evening out with her friends. She could take off any time and return at her leisure just so long as as she told Sara of her whereabouts. Although Parviz was against the purchase of the car, he knew Sara wouldn't listen to him.

She never had. The same way she'd never cut back on her phone conversations. When he was growing up in Tabriz, his mother rarely used the phone, and if she did, it was only in the mornings when his father was at work. The telephone was for emergencies, and if anybody called in the evenings, it was usually for his father. In the '70s it wasn't customary for people to pick up the phone and idly chat away their precious time and hard-earned money. Parviz was keenly aware of how times had changed. Sara and Mina acted as if they couldn't separate from their cell phones; they were their lifelines.

How Sara was able to have so many friends, and to keep up with them, was a mystery to Parviz. He was never an outgoing soul. Finding friends was particularly difficult for him, although he'd gradually become better at it. Even at fifty-two, he still felt pretty awkward meeting new people, let alone talking to them on the phone. He didn't even have much to say to his sister, who occasionally called from Tabriz. Or to his brother in London, who contacted him maybe once a year. Sara and Mina checked their cell phone every few seconds as if verifying their very existence. They were never separated from their phones, even taking them to the bed with them. Sara placed hers on the nightstand, while Mina put hers under her pillow. Without their cell phones, they felt lost and disconnected. Parviz had refused to have a cell phone in spite of their insistence. He relied on the landline at home, but nobody ever called for him anyway.

It was Sara who had accumulated more and more friends through the years. She had a score of classmates from high school. Then her college cohort was added to her circle when she got her bachelor's, not to mention additional groups with each post-graduate degree she earned. People from her Master's degree, and more recently, her Ph.D. colleagues had joined the group when she started her teaching job at the university; relatives and neighbors were already there. Her new book club contacts were welcomed like old friends.

"You never know," she repeatedly told Parviz. "Tomorrow you'll need a doctor. Or I want to remodel the kitchen. We need people who can help."

But Parviz was fine in his quiet world, never feeling a particular need to make friends. For him, it was absolutely unnecessary to invite colleagues or friends to the house.

"Why don't you invite the new engineer in your firm," Sara asked him more than once, apparently eager to add him to her list of friends.

"I will, I will," Parviz told her. "He's very busy right now, I am sure. You know, getting adjusted and all that."

"Why, that's more reason to extend an invitation. To welcome him to your firm. You could invite your boss too. We can give an office party."

Nodding in silence, Parviz picked up the evening newspaper on the coffee table, hiding his face behind it. He had no interest inviting total strangers to his home, no matter how much Sara insisted.

Early in their marriage, Parviz had realized that every connection turned into a lasting relationship for Sara. Every time he turned his head, she was talking to a new friend. He could no longer keep track of who was who. Perplexed by this peculiar ability of hers, he wondered what propelled Sara to make so many friends and to run such long conversations on the phone. Were they really her friends as she claimed? He had a feeling Sara shared everything with them, even details of their private life. But he didn't want to dwell much on that possibility.

With time his initial surprise turned into a deep irritation, for he realized no topic of discussion was ever overlooked in her phone conversations. The moment somebody found out which store had diapers, Sara's friends called each other, and everybody went shopping for diapers. Of course, those were the times of scarcity and serious shortage of everything in the market due to the war with Iraq and economic embargo. Parviz initially thought those conversations would eventually come to an end. But much to his dismay, even after goods became more available, the chitchat continued. What party to go to, which fridge to purchase, where to buy facial lotion or wax their legs were recurrent topics of deep and intense discussion. Hair salons were also a favorite topic. Holding the evening newspaper in front of him, he often realized that all he was doing was listening to Sara's phone conversation.

"Did you know the guy who owned the Balenciaga hair salon now works at home? I love it. I missed him so much when beauty salons operated by men were banned. I didn't know where to go for a simple haircut, let alone color. Men stylists are the best. Like men tailors. My best tailor left the country. I have tried so many women, but nobody is as good as my Armenian tailor."

Parviz didn't know how many times he had heard similar comments. He grew totally disappointed in Sara's persistent waste of time. His conclusion was that there was an innate female trait to talk nonstop about trivial things. He couldn't even recall the first names of his colleagues, people he saw every day, while Sara remembered all her friends' birthdays, and the birthdays of their children.

§

"Are you on the phone again?" Parviz asked angrily upon entering the house.

Sara nodded. She normally paid no attention to his tone or to his words.

"Fun chatting with you, Layla. I have to go, but will call you soon."

As if she hadn't even noticed his objection, she turned to Parviz excitedly, "Layla's brother is moving to Canada. Their visa has come. The whole family is leaving. He already has a job lined up for him. In an engineering firm."

Looking at Sara in bafflement, Parviz wondered why she never stopped telling him about all the people who were leaving the country left and right. He knew she wanted to go too, harboring her own dreams of a better future for Mina, for their family. For herself. She was tired of being confined, frustrated that her expertise was being wasted because of limited research opportunities. She watched her young students sadly, fully conscious that a majority of them wouldn't be able to use their knowledge in a useful way. Sara had no interest in staying put while Parviz was steadfast about serving the country, educating the next generation, no matter what challenges they might endure. So many had escaped after the revolution that the entire city looked different the first ten years. Parviz had no interest in emigrating, making his position as clear as he could to Sara. As far as he was concerned, those who left were traitors.

Ignoring her comment, he changed before going to the yard to water the thirsty flowerbeds. He craved that special scent of wet earth that wafted from the ground the moment he opened the hose and watered not only his garden but also the brick pathways. He wanted to feel the warm water sitting in the hose gradually turning cool as it ran, soaking his feet, calming his nerves.

Pouring two cups of tea, Sara followed Parviz to the yard. Waiting for him to change the hose from his right hand to the left, she handed him the teacup.

"I was at the Canadian Embassy today," she said calmly.

Parviz stayed quiet, not turning his head to face her.

"They need more documents: affidavit and official translations of our birth certificates. It seems things are finally working out." Pausing for a second, she slowly added, "They are looking for people like us."

"This country needs us, too," Parviz said, trying to control his temper. "This poor land, these poor people need us more than any other country."

Determined to avoid another argument, Sara kept her voice steady, "I just wanted to let you know that things are working out, but we don't need to tell anybody yet."

"What about your parents? Or my mother?" Parviz asked. "Who's going to take care of them if something happens? They aren't getting any younger."

"I'm concerned about them as much as you are, but we'll think about that when the time comes. At this point, we need to save ourselves. We have a daughter to think about," Sara said.

"Do whatever you want," were Parviz's last words before he walked to the flowerbeds at the end of the yard, pulling the hose behind him. He wanted to think that as a couple, they had no serious conflict, just disagreements. He wanted to believe that holding different opinions was only a natural part of marriage.

Throwing her tea in the flowerbed, Sara turned back to the house. They didn't mention immigration any more at dinner, both seemingly lost in their own thoughts. Sara was reviewing the paperwork she needed to do. Parviz kept quiet as usual, wondering if the wrong birthday date he had put on his application made a difference.

§

Parviz was an excellent student all his life. Back in high school, he studied math because his older siblings majored in math. His scores were so high in the national entrance exam that he automatically got admitted to the best school.

"I can take care of your registration, get you signed up for civil engineering," Rahman, his brother who was a senior, told him. "Civil is a good field; you can always find a job with it."

"Sure, that would be fine," Parviz said excitedly. At seventeen, he didn't have a clear idea what he wanted to study anyway.

"Maybe we can open our own firm after you graduate," Rahman had added enthusiastically.

A job prospect even before starting college! Parviz felt elated about the possibility of starting a company with his brother.

That evening Rahman told Parviz, "Well, civil was already full so I signed you up for electrical." And Parviz accepted that, too. Engineering was engineering, and the specialty did not matter to him at the time. He was just happy to go to the same university as his brother. Because of his high math scores, everybody expected him to study engineering. It was only years later that he regretted his decision, wishing he had studied humanities, perhaps art. He was good at math, but his heart was into the fields that touched the soul. Exactly the type of areas that were totally unacceptable for his family and most of the people they knew. Studying electrical engineering had been a mistake, and now even the prospect of going to Canada, a dream Sara cherished, sounded detestable to him.

§

As a successful engineer, Parviz had become more daring with his personal interests. Most of his colleagues played bridge once a week; the game was the high point of their week, and nothing interrupted it—not even when the revolutionary government banned all card games. But Parviz wasn't interested in cards; he had his secret fascination with music, especially piano. Hearing his colleagues chat about a piano teacher, he was intrigued. Taking private lessons appealed to him. He was thirty; it was either now or never. He found out the teacher was an Armenian woman who gave private lessons and allowed the students to stay for thirty minutes to practice for free. He liked the arrangement; he'd go there for a thirty-minute lesson once a week, practice a bit, and go back to work. Nobody would find out about it.

But it took him a long time to gather the courage to make an appointment. He had gone to her address in Shemiran, checking the house several times, hoping to get a sense of the people living there. He never saw anybody going in or coming out, but he could often hear the sound of Western classical music floating from one of the second floor windows. The house looked big like any other in that neighborhood, except for a small front garden with different exotic plants that separated it from the street by a tall white iron fence.

The first time Parviz rang the doorbell, he was full of apprehension, prepared to walk away quickly, but before he could, an older woman stepped out of the building to open the door. Looking at him suspiciously, she stood behind the iron door, waiting for him to speak, but he had lost his speech. Stepping back awkwardly, he just looked at her, taken aback by her deep blue eyes and uncovered unruly hair. Impatient with his visible discomfort, she finally said, "You're here for piano lessons?" Surprised by her thick accent, he politely nodded.

She stepped aside to make room for him to enter, but she didn't volunteer any small talk. He followed her as she motioned him toward the house. Walking a few steps, he found himself facing a very tall, elaborately carved wooden door. He had never seen such an ornate entry. Stepping into the building, his vision went dark. He needed a few seconds to get used to the dim hallway. He paused a long moment, afraid of walking blindly. Turning back, the woman looked at him, puzzled by his delay. Cautiously inching forward, he saw daylight beaming in at the end of the hallway where there seemed to be a living room. He could see a couple of chairs.

Reaching inside the threshold of the room, the woman stopped. "Mrs. Petrosian will be with you presently," she said before leaving him alone in the middle of a huge dining room. The room was furnished with handcrafted built-in wood cabinets. The table sat at least sixteen, if not more. Looking into the adjoining living room, he noticed a piano next to a glass wall that opened to the backyard. Glancing around, he didn't know what to do. Look at the original watercolors on the wall or the antiques in the ornate china cabinet? He didn't step on the pair of Persian carpets that covered the central space, leaving parts of the marble floor revealed. He had never seen such an exquisite living room, such beautiful silk carpets. They must have been specifically ordered for this room, he thought.

The Victorian furniture spoke of wealth, status, sophistication. Carefully walking to the piano, he saw a swimming pool surrounded by flowering irises and narcissus; the mass of purplish blue was breathtaking. Mesmerized by the late spring flowers, he only gradually sensed another presence in the room. Turning away from the glass wall, his eyes met a short heavyset woman looking at him.

"Such a beautiful house," was all he could mutter.

"Yes, it belongs to my father-in-law. He built it in the 50's."

"Those irises!"

"Ayame. That's what they are called. Japanese. They love dry soil."

He introduced himself, wondering whether he should shake hands. She did not offer her hand.

"So, you want to play piano?" Mrs. Petrosian asked, slowly walking toward the piano.

"Yes, but I have never played any instrument." There was no way to hide his ignorance.

"What do you do?" she asked. "Your occupation?"

"I am an engineer."

"Well, that's a good starting point," she said with a faint smile. "Learning to play piano is like any other skill. It takes time and perseverance."

"I just want to learn the notes. Perhaps to read sheet music. Maybe play a song or two. I know it's too late to start at my age."

"It's never too late to learn. Anybody can learn. Like anybody can sing, but not everybody becomes a famous singer." He liked her direct words, encouraging yet honest.

It was the first time he was telling a woman—a total stranger—that he would love to play music. It felt like the biggest confession of his life. Light and humble, that's how he felt.

Ringing the doorbell to that house became the high point of his week, the moment he awaited for from week to week. Once inside, he was all ears, listening to the sound of a different language coming from the second floor while he rarely got a glimpse of the people who spoke it. The classical music from the second floor spread throughout the house, creating a calming atmosphere. Like a child, Parviz saw that house as a closed universe, a wonderland, a place he knew not many Muslims had ever entered. He wondered about the family's background. Were they turn of the century refugees, escaping Armenian genocide in Turkey? Had they come from Russia? Were they among the Armenians who had arrived in Iran in the 17th century? Questions floated in his mind, but a half hour of weekly lessons did not offer an opportunity for such conversations. Thirsty for learning, that's how he felt.

§

Mrs. Petrosian's teaching fascinated him. She always started by playing a short piece on the phonograph, emphasizing that he needed to learn to listen to music, to hear the rhythm, melody, and texture. She took out her records one by one without touching their surface, handling them so delicately as if they were rare silk. Hearing Chopin's sonatas, she asked, what thoughts or feelings did the music create in him. He fell in love with Franz Liszt piano sonata the first time he heard it, captivated by its slow beginning, repetition of rhythmic gypsy melodies, and rich emotional assaults. It touched his soul, perhaps because of the simultaneous familiar and unfamiliar melodies Liszt so masterfully had interwoven. He couldn't even imagine what thoughts or emotions led a composer to create such a masterpiece filled with emotional turmoil.

As she taught him the basic notes, he listened attentively. Noticing her long and strong fingers over the keyboard, he realized how inflexible his own fingers were. Eager for his weekly lessons, he nevertheless felt utterly inadequate. For the first time, he doubted his intelligence. He had never felt slow or clueless about learning. He had mastered the toughest topics in college with no trouble at all, but he was now struggling over the most basic notes. He was embarrassed about his inability to learn the lessons the first, second, or even the third time. His fingers on the piano keys froze and turned into short, flat wooden sticks. He distrusted his hearing, unable to discern the difference between the notes. But the experience of taking lessons and learning something new was so satisfying that he willingly accepted his inadequacy. The lessons had given him a second life, a new hidden energy source that thrilled him.

He attributed his interest to her teaching. Mrs. Petrosian was a serene and poised woman, never tiring of repeating the same lesson again and again. Not even a slight sign of impatience appeared on her face. Picking up the least trace of confusion in his frowned eyebrows, she would tell him, "Excellence comes with practice, with time, with perseverance." He wondered about her wisdom—was it cultivated or an innate ability. He tried to rationalize her understanding, telling himself, "She needs private students." He was paying handsomely for his lessons, but the lessons had fulfilled a deep-felt desire in him. There was something special about Mrs. Petrosian's teaching. He had never had a teacher like her. The vague sadness in her large black eyes had a calming effect on him. He knew she wouldn't be asking any personal questions. Their half hour was devoted to learning and listening.

He wanted nothing more than continuing his lessons, nothing more than entering that calm space that separated him from the rest of his mundane life.

§

Maybe he should have known. Maybe he knew but didn't want to accept the reality. People were leaving the country in droves. "Anything is better than staying here," he kept hearing. One of his colleagues had already left for Turkey. Nobody had known about his plans to leave the country. One day he didn't show up, and it was only after a number of phone calls that they discovered his whereabouts.

"Thank goodness he's not in prison for his ideas, but why did he escape like a criminal?" Parviz asked the two co-owners of the company. "He couldn't even let us know? As if we would give him away?"

Looking at each other, one of the owners said, "There is no trust anymore. People are scared." The other went to his office and closed the door.

There were signs everywhere. He saw parents resorting to any means to get their sons out of the country to escape military service. One paid an exorbitant amount to get his seventeen-year-old escape through Pakistan in sheep's skin. Entire families left, leaving their houses and belongings behind. Many didn't utter a word to their friends, neighbors, or colleagues; some escaped because of the raging war, others because of the new regime.

Going to work one Monday morning, he found that the door was locked. When he rang the doorbell, nobody answered. He didn't know what to do. Go back home or wait by the door? What if the firm's partners had been picked up by the revolutionary guards? They always gave big parties, and men and women freely intermingled, with the women showing their hair as if they were still living under the Shah's rule. He had regularly turned down their invitation with lame excuses, in spite of Sara's insistence that they should go.

He was certain his bosses had been arrested for throwing these mixed parties and serving alcohol. As he was imagining the worst scenarios, he suddenly spotted Shahin, one of the owners, crossing the street.

"Where is Hooshang? Why is the door is locked? Even Mohammad the custodian isn't here."

"I am here," Shahin said quietly, "come in."

It was only after closing the door behind them that Parviz found out that Hooshang had left the country over the weekend. He was joining his wife and children who, apparently, had already gone in Canada.

"We are closing the firm," Shahin said, avoiding eye contact. Putting his hand on Parviz's shoulder, Shahin said in a fatherly tone, "You should leave too. There is nothing left for us in this country except fear and pain. I can't sleep at nights, am scared for my son, for my daughters, for my wife. Even a thirteen-year-old boy can insult my fifty-year-old wife, pointing a machine gun at her in the middle of the night, ordering her to cover her hair."

"Are you leaving too?" Parviz asked, sounding weak.

Looking at him pensively, he responded, "I have no choice."

"But who is going to rebuild this country if people like you leave?"

"There was a time I thought we could do something. There was a moment of hope, of trust," Shahin said, shaking his head. "No longer."

Noticing the distressed look on his employee's face, Shahin added, "Who knows? I may come back in a year or two if the situation gets better, but I doubt my wife would ever come back. We'll see."

Looking at his desk, Parviz didn't see anything of value to take home with him.

§

The loss of his job meant the end of piano lessons for Parviz.

Sara had never found out about his clandestine piano classes. Never noticed the mysterious smile that started to appear on his thin lips. Neither did she see the magic in his eyes. The musical notes he started whistling escaped her attention. Subtly tapping his fingertips on the steering wheel or the newspaper didn't seem worthy of attention. Absorbed in her own life, Sara failed to see her husband's newfound energy, and its eventual abrupt expiration.

That was the point when Parviz could no longer oppose Sara's plans for moving to Canada. They had three months to leave the country, Sara told him one afternoon. He could no longer argue on behalf of the young nation that needed their expertise, or the elderly parents who were going to be left alone. Sara had made no secret of her plans.

Unemployed, Parviz felt forced to surrender to Sara's plans for them. He was angry at himself, at his colleagues, at Sara, at life.

"We'll give it a try," he said reluctantly.

§

Parviz didn't even want to think how he had survived his long years of exile, living like an outcast in Regina, Saskatchewan. Alas, he couldn't even remember the name of the province, let alone pronouncing it. He had never felt so lonely, so useless in his life, so depressed. Before Canada, he didn't know what it meant to be depressed. Now he knew.

"What are we doing in this country?" he asked Sara repeatedly. "Why did you want to leave Iran? Why should we serve another country? All the doctors and engineers have moved to Canada while there is a shortage of physicians and engineers in Iran."

"It's not my fault if everybody has fled the country," Sara responded dismissively.

Parvis had never understood Sara's ambitions, her blind desire to move abroad, to live a life different from millions of others.

"What's wrong with Iran?" he insisted, knowing too well that it was a rhetorical rather than a genuine question. He knew the answer, but he believed that if others suffered, they should suffer with them. They had everything in Iran—family, money, status—but Sara was still unhappy with the life they had made there.

What was this insatiable hunger to live in the West? In a town nobody had heard of, he thought angrily.

Iran was his country; he knew the people, loved the culture. Parviz resented living in Regina, remaining a foreigner for the rest of his life. His accented English transformed him into an uneducated man every time he opened his mouth. Worse, his thirteen-year-old daughter had started correcting his English in public, as though she were embarrassed by the way he talked, by the way he walked, by the way he dressed. He could see her cringing when he spoke up in public, when he picked her up at school. Mina was quickly losing her childhood, turning into a teenager, supposedly more knowledgeable than her father. She was becoming an accent-less Canadian while Parviz was turning into a burden on his family.

A nobody, that's who he had become.

"I don't want to live like an alien, like an outcast," he told Sara. "We'll never belong to this country."

"As if we are not outcasts in Iran?" Sara said. Looking at him angrily, she asked, "Which is worse? Being a foreigner in a foreign country or turning into a foreigner in your own?"

§

Sara had found a job quickly. Her chemical engineering degree made her marketable. She liked her job, the fact that they valued her knowledge, that there were opportunities for advancement. Her big source of worry was Parviz, who was becoming more withdrawn day by day. She returned home after work, only to find Parviz on the couch, reading Hafez, reciting centuries old poetry to himself. Not moving an inch since she had left in the morning. She kept hoping that once he found a job, he'd adjust. But Parviz wasn't interested in the job search; he saw their stay as temporary.

Sara was becoming more quiet, too, tired of having a conversation in the evenings. She found herself reading Persian novels at nights as if searching for an answer. She missed home, the comfortable life she had back in Tehran—a maid who cooked and cleaned daily, the male servant who helped with spring cleaning, window washing, and big parties. No, she didn't want to deal with the veil and new regulations about proper conduct for women, but she missed her luxurious life, the fact that she never thought about money, that she could purchase anything she fancied. Life in Regina had proven to be centered on work, work, and more work.

Nobody called her Dr. Mahdavi since they had moved. She was a lab technician with no title. Everybody called her by her first name.

When she told her boss that they were going back, he told her they'd keep her job for a while just in case she changed her mind. Sara felt disheartened about leaving Regina, unable to share the joy other passengers expressed the night the plane landed in Tehran's airport. She was torn having to choose between two worlds, but she couldn't see herself as a mere lab technician for the rest of her life.

§

All Parviz cared about was that he was back in Tehran. He had missed the sun, the heat, the traffic, the noisy life that never stopped. The night the plane landed at Mehrabad airport, Parviz couldn't wait to breathe the warm, dry air of the city, smelling of diesel. The August heat wave calmed his over-stimulated nerves. Fortunately, they had only rented out their house and could easily move back in. The country was slowly recuperating, as if waking up from a disturbing slumber. The situation seemed more stable; there were brand new cars in the streets, shops carrying more goods, store owners willing to sell their goods instead of hiding them in their back rooms, selling only to their preferred customers. The era of reform had started, delivering new hope. Parviz felt invigorated, more than ready to dive back into the world of work. People were starting new companies, and were interested in hiring him, especially with his three years of life abroad. Parviz quickly got a job, but he was surprised to hear that some of his former colleagues had returned home without their wife and children. That seemed to be the new lifestyle: wife and children living abroad while the husbands had returned home to work to support their families. He was so happy they had returned as an intact family, no ocean separating them. Sara went back to her professorship at the university. With more students, there was a higher need for teachers. Her students were calling her Professor again. It sounded good, the echo satisfying her ego. She had gained her title again, and with her stint in Canada, she hoped to chair the chemistry department soon.

Finding a job, shopping at the same old grocery stores, speaking a language everyone understood, listening to the taxi drivers and shop owners talk politics, bringing his mother to live with them—all in all gave him a sense of vitality, a new zeal for life. Parviz felt connected and useful again.

Picking up his old habits with a new zest, Parviz walked to most places. Sara dropped him off in the mornings, and he walked back home, often exploring new building construction on his way. Everybody was building. Some because Saddam Hussein's bombing had destroyed their homes. Others because real estate had skyrocketed. One or two story houses were being turned into six or eight story apartment complexes in all neighborhoods. The population growth demanded the new construction.

The uneven sidewalks or hungry cats searching in the garbage didn't bother Parviz. The maddening traffic and angry drivers did not disturb him. He loved the aroma of fresh bread wafting from the neighborhood bakeries. Walking by the market, he enjoyed the image of piled up ripe and juicy fruits. He stood behind the window of the flower shops, closing his eyes, taking deep breath to get a full sense of tuberose, lilies, and roses. The combined scents of flowers and the cool air escaping from the shop was enough to intoxicate him, transporting him into a love garden only hinted at in a *Thousand and One Nights*.

It was on one of those excursions that he found himself in Mrs. Petrosian's neighborhood, and finally on their street. It was at that moment that he realized how badly he wanted to continue his lessons. Counting his steps, he could hear Liszt's "Hungarian Rhapsody" clearly. He told himself that he just wanted to see the house, listen for a fleeting moment to the music from the second-floor window. From a distance, he could hear the ear piercing sound of construction and trucks dumping piles of brick and rebar on the street. The trucks had blocked the sidewalk and stopped traffic. As he got closer, he doubted he was on the right street. Reaching the construction area, all he saw was a huge void in the place where Mrs. Petrosian's house was supposed to be. A big hole in the ground. No signs of her house tucked in between other houses, no iron fence or the small exotic front garden. No music coming from the second floor window. Only the deafening noise of the trucks. The gray sky and the dust rising from the construction made the gap deeper, uglier. Parviz just stood there.

"We're ready for presale," Parviz heard a voice. Dumbfounded, he turned to see a young man dressed in a white pressed Calvin Klein shirt.

"Are you interested in buying? They are going to be beautiful. Two or three bedrooms with two penthouses on the top floor. Swimming pool and sauna in the basement."

"What happened to the family who lived here?"

"Why, they sold their house," the man said joyfully. "Wonderful location for luxury flats. Only two units on each floor."

"But why?"

Looking at him curiously, the man said, "They were sitting on a gold mine with no cash to mine the gold."

"But this was a historic house. Like a museum, part of our history."

"You know how much it cost them to just water their garden?" the man chuckled.

Parviz remembered the rows of irises, Japanese quince, snowberry bush. The covered terrace housed many bonsais in oval or rectangular pots. He had never seen such tiny little trees.

Noticing the stunned look on his face, the man added, "They have left the country." As he turned on his heels, he paused, and gave him his business card. "Let me know if you're interested. These will be gone before you know."

"Where have they gone?"

"Where everybody else is going. Canada, Germany, Australia. Wherever they can. Who wouldn't leave if they could?"

Second Marriage

RIDING THE BUS, Soheil kept staring at the dry landscape speeding by. He had taken this trip numerous times in his life, and he looked forward to seeing the first tree, a lone evergreen, when they rounded the curve. It was in a small oasis farther down the road. Then, right before reaching the mountaintop, he would watch the scenery slowly change from a drab, desert-like, all-enveloping ochre, to an expanded pistachio-colored rice field. Finally at the mountaintop, a whole new expanse would reveal a plush view. The closer he got, the more alert he felt, anxious to get a glimpse of the Caspian Sea, taking in its white-capped waves from afar, hearing its music in his heart in spite of the distance. Just hours out of Tehran, a luscious tropical forest welcomed him back.

Even though he loved going home, he always felt apprehensive about the mountain road, which was well known as a deathtrap. There were horror stories of chain-reaction crashes along the blind turns—buses losing control, trucks going down the cliff, spring avalanches blocking the road. He couldn't wait for the bus to reach the top. The driver was pushing heavily on the gas pedal. Sometimes Soheil was afraid that the bus wouldn't be able to pull its weight up the steep road. Drifting into a pleasant stupor during his last trip, he had been woken by the sound of other passengers praying out loud for a safe passage. There was a complete whiteout; a heavy fog had descended on the road. Hardly able to see a meter ahead, the driver had called on the passengers to pray. To calm their nerves, the travelers had obliged. Joining the others, Soheil had added his own pray for a safe passage, holding tight to his rosary.

§

This time, Soheil was going home to do all the talking himself.

His family had taken care of everything the first time he wanted to marry. Everybody had been looking forward to Soheil and Jasmin's wedding; they had known each other from childhood, gone to the same school, sat next to each other in the classroom, walked back home together. Soheil had known how bright she was, for they did their homework together. More significantly, Jasmin's family was much better off than his, and he had definitely wanted to marry a girl who was wealthy, educated, and outgoing. Suffering a life of privation, Soheil had been determined to make a successful living for himself and to provide a decent life for his family. He had given his mother Ziba and five sisters absolute authority to make all the arrangements in his absence while he stayed at work in Tehran. Their marriage had been blessed by both families, with the elders giving their consent a long time before, and the young looking forward to a big celebration.

It would be different with Pari, however. Unlike the first time, Soheil knew he needed to talk to her without any intermediary.

§

"Would you like me to ask for Pari's hand the way we did it last time?" Ziba had casually asked, careful not to mention Jasmin's name. "You know when we were kids, we always played at their house. They had

134

the biggest orchard. Pari's mother Layla and I were inseparable as kids. She knows you're interested in Pari."

"No, thank you mother. I need to talk to Pari myself. I'll do it the next time I am visiting."

Worried about her only son's future, Ziba switched into a monologue about her childhood games at Layla's parents.

"You never saw their orchard; we had so much fun playing there. Boys and girls together. There were orange trees in the back, tangerines in the front, and bitter oranges right by the entrance. In the front, they had planted honeysuckle bushes that covered the entire clay wall," Ziba said. "Pari's mother loved flowering bushes, especially roses and orange azalea mixed in a background of forsythia. Her winter heath started blooming in the fall. I wish you had seen her garden before they sold most of the orchard. Now it's just block after block of apartments."

Soheil listened patiently. Ziba loved to talk about her childhood memories as if her entire life was encapsulated in those years.

"We played hide and seek behind the hydrangea bushes. I had discovered an old pomegranate tree in the very back of the garden. I could climb up easily; nobody ever found me there. They'd look for me everywhere, called my name several times, and I wouldn't come out from my secret spot." Without a pause, Ziba continued, "By the way, your sister, Mehri, can talk to Pari if that's all right with you. They are seeing each other this Friday, going to the market."

Another kind and not so subtle motherly suggestion, Soheil thought to himself. He trusted his mother and knew that she wouldn't do anything against his will, but things were different this time. He had to act independently, knowing that Pari was concerned with some issues he couldn't understand. She had shown her doubts through vague or abrupt questions during their long distance phone conversations. Soheil felt ill at ease; he had already visited her family formally. But he couldn't understand Pari's reasons for being reserved, as if she was suffering from some doubts. Pari was never explicit enough, prefacing everything with, "My grandmother says this …" or "My aunt thinks that …" Was she hiding behind what others supposedly said? He didn't know. But he couldn't believe that Pari's entire family would be concerned about their future marriage. He concluded to himself that maybe women suffered from some innate feeling of insecurity.   Reluctant to ignore Pari's doubtful remarks, Soheil decided it was unwise to make definite plans before all the uncertainties were resolved.

Soheil wanted to have a fresh start, free of doubts and concerns.

§

Having lived in Tehran for several years, Soheil could choose a wife among his colleagues or his old college friends, but he was determined to marry a woman who knew him and his family. Preferably a distant cousin who could sympathize with him. He believed a girl from Tehran would never understand what he had gone through.

After he lost his first wife, he had actually decided never to marry again. His grief was immense, stabbing him in the chest in the middle of the night, leaving him wide awake, both unable and reluctant to brush away the sweet thought of Jasmin. Only if he had acted a couple weeks earlier, even a few days, Jasmin would be alive, and his life would have been entirely different.

"When we grow up, we'll be husband and wife," he remembered announcing to Jasmin when he was only seven years old. He couldn't wait to grow up faster, asking his mother every few months, "How old am I now?"

Knowing well why Soheil kept asking such a question, Ziba humored her only son, "You're old, very old, but not old enough to marry your sweetheart."

"How long do I have to wait, then?"

"A bit longer, God willing. I'll let you know as soon as you're ready."

And Soheil kept waiting for the right day. He was the only student in his entire village who was admitted to the university in Tehran. Moving to the capital proved to be quite an adventure, but his heart and mind stayed behind in his village near Manjil, with Jasmin. There were so many Tehrani girls in college, the kind of girls he had never met before. They talked to guys, dressed in totally different outfits compared to his sisters and other women in the village. Tehran was almost like a different country. He saw women professors, women counselors, women doctors. There were no women dentists in his village, but he had gone to a woman dentist for a root canal in Tehran. A number of his professors at the university were women. And that was in 1985, only a few years after the revolution, when many professional women were sent home, or as some said, encouraged to retire early.

His love for Jasmin did not fade away with the distance between them. If anything, the separation and homesickness intensified his devotion. But adulthood had created new boundaries and new restrictions. If, as children, they went to the same school and sat next to each other, they could no longer freely see each other. That was totally inappropriate. Unrelated men and women did not spend time alone together in his village. In Tehran, many of his classmates found their spouses in school. Although Soheil's classmates were extremely careful because of the new revolutionary zeal, the possibility of meeting strangers did still exist in college. But back in his village, there was no opportunity for Soheil and Jasmin to get together alone, maybe drive to Roodbar, the nearest city, for an afternoon stroll or lunch. If such outings had become a possibility in the '70s before the revolution, they had become an impossibility in the '80s.

Going home to visit his family, Soheil hoped to get a glimpse of Jasmin in the alley, or perhaps at the Friday market. Maybe he'd see her when he was standing by the door, chatting with his friends, prolonging a goodbye, exchanging a neighborly greeting. People always wanted to know about Tehran, and dropped by when he visited. All his sisters came for a visit, and they stayed at their parents' house as long as Soheil did. Their house became like a kindergarten, with all five sisters bringing their children. Fortunately, the sisters were a fountain of information about Jasmin. His love was no family secret.

"Jasmin looks prettier every day," his youngest sister, Nadereh, would say.

"I heard she has a new suitor," Mehri said teasingly, adding after a pause, "but she keeps turning everybody down. She's waiting for the right man."

"She was asking about you the other day, wondering if you'll be here for the New Year," Nadereh said playfully.

And with that comment, Soheil felt elated. If Jasmin was directly asking about him, life could not get any better. He felt safe and secure believing that Jasmin would wait for him to get a job and save some money. He couldn't rely on his father to assist him with starting his own family, maybe helping with the rent or other expenses. He didn't want to be a burden, knowing well that his family barely met their own needs. He wanted to do everything properly, to find a secure job and provide decently for his family before formally asking for Jasmin's hand.

Unlike Soheil, Jasmin had grown up in comfort. Her father, Mr. Zamani, had a pomegranate orchard and rich rice fields. Soheil's father, Majid, on the other hand, was a manual laborer, having to spend months at a time in Tehran without seeing his family. Majid never held on to any of his jobs for long because he missed Ziba and his six children. He often left whatever job he had without a word of notice, catching the last bus for Manjil, appearing at his family's house in the middle of the night. He spent a few weeks with his children before taking off again in the wee hours of the morning. Majid was a source of joy when visiting; he was a bundle of affection, showering his children with love and tenderness. But his interrupted work meant the family didn't have much to live by from month to month. In his absence, Ziba was the head of the family. She had become the disciplinarian, raising six children almost on her own. Soheil admired his father, but he always thought that Majid's love for his family had prevented him from adequately providing for them. He was determined to be a prosperous man.

§

Soheil landed a nice job right after he graduated. Although the pay wasn't as high as he wanted, he was at least a salaried man now, hired by the government, which offered the most secure jobs, with many fringe benefits. His news of getting a stable job was the joyous moment everybody was waiting for at home. And that's when he told Ziba to act on his behalf and ask for Jasmin's hand in his absence, instructing her to accept any conditions her family posed.

Ziba bought boxes of sweets from Roodbar, wrapped yards of beautiful silk fabric Soheil had sent from Tehran as a present for Jasmin's mother and sisters, invited a few family elders, and paid a formal visit to Jasmin's family.

Although the Zamani's were much better off, they happily agreed to the marriage, not demanding an unreasonable dowry or pushing for unfair conditions. The family was going to lose their daughter because Jasmin would be living in Tehran with Soheil, but that was acceptable because they knew she had been waiting for this moment for years.

Soheil's time away in college had been particularly difficult for Jasmin; she had expressed serious concern to Soheil's sisters, veiled in vague questions and pointed comments about losing him to Tehrani girls. But Soheil had proven to be steadfast in his dedication to his first childhood love. Yes, there were many girls in college to choose from, but Soheil was madly in love with only one girl, and he knew the only way to have her would be by finishing college and getting a good job. And that he had done dutifully.

§

Soheil could hear the excitement in his mother's voice when he picked up the phone. "Everything is settled, the date of the wedding, the dowry, the list of guests, the dishes we are going to make," Ziba exclaimed in one breath.

Before Ziba could utter the next sentence, Mehri grabbed the phone from her mother and added laughingly, "You should have been there.

Jasmin's father's gave a long speech about what a good marriage entails, but at the end he listed all the presents he's going to give you two."

Soheil respected Mr. Zamani greatly. He had worked for him during the last years of his high school, and the old man had paid him generously. Although he wanted to stay in the village after he graduated from high school, both Majid and Mr. Zamani encouraged him to leave for Tehran.

Mr. Zamani had pulled him aside when he heard Soheil was accepted to college, and told him, "Son, I have faith in you. Go to college. Get your degree. You'll be the first in your family to have college education. The first in this village. You'll make all of us proud."

Soheil could barely hide his happiness, his immense satisfaction at receiving so much support and encouragement.

§

The two families set the wedding date for June 24. Soheil had given them a small window in June to pick a date; his boss wanted him back at work five days after.

Much had to be arranged before he could bring Jasmin to Tehran. The most important was moving to a two-bedroom apartment instead of the single room he had rented for the last five years. His two oldest sisters traveled to Tehran to help him with the move and wedding preparations. He took them to the store whose window he had spent hours in front of, looking at different beautiful wedding gowns, not daring to step inside all by himself. He had dreamed about buying Jasmin's dress from Tehran. They had already gone to the Grand Bazaar to buy a gold ring and bracelets for her. Overwhelmed by the shining gold all around them, it took the three of them more than one trip to decide what to buy.

"This is Tehran after all," Soheil kept reminding them, "very different from our village and Roodbar." Tradition dictated that the mother of the bride receive a nice present, so they bought her a lovely gold pendent. Surrounded by what seemed like a sea of gold, Soheil's sisters could not resist buying themselves a couple of bracelets. "It's a festive time," Soheil told them, encouraging their extravagance.

Finally, Soheil's new apartment was nicely furnished with the furniture that Jasmin's father sent as part of his wedding present. His sisters went back home, taking the wedding gown and the numerous presents they had bought, delighted to have helped him with his preparations. Soheil kept the wedding ring though, hiding it in his pillowcase. At nights before falling sleep, he'd take the ring out, touching the beautiful, shiny gold, pressing his thumb on the single diamond on the ring, dreaming about the day he'd put it on Jasmin's delicate hand. Only three more weeks, and a lifetime of waiting would end. Finally they'd be living together, under the same roof. Finally.

Soheil felt exuberant, and he walked taller, lighter, and more confidently every day.

§

But that was not all; there was more to think about and to plan. He had decided it would be best for Jasmin to get a two-year degree in order to find a job. Jasmin had shown interest in medical school, but Soheil didn't think that was a good idea. It was too demanding for a woman to become a doctor; instead he'd encourage her to get a teaching job, preferably at the elementary level. That would be more proper for her. It would be good for Jasmin to teach, to meet other women, to become familiar with the people and customs of Tehran. Everything was so different in Tehran; men and women colleagues became friends. They chatted and laughed together comfortably. That would be very strange for Jasmin.

His friend Sima came to his mind—her vibrating voice, and her caramel color skin. At first he couldn't believe Sima was Iranian, assuming everybody in the country had skin as light as his fellow-villagers. He kept waiting for her real skin color to show, for the suntan to go away, but Sima didn't change color even during cold winter months.

Sima and Soheil had met in college. Coming from smaller cities with no relatives in Tehran, they had become good friends in no time. While Soheil was from the North, Sima had come from the most southern part of the country, where the African and Arab influence was strong and visible. It was her color and her slight accent, especially the way she pronounced certain words, that unconsciously drew Soheil to her. Her small shapely nose, jet-black straight hair, and large dreamy eyes that always hid a puzzling smile were a source of curiosity to him. Upon graduation, Sima moved back to her hometown, but when Soheil's boss asked him if he could recommend somebody for the new opening they had, Soheil immediately suggested Sima. Their friendship only deepened when Sima and her husband moved to the city.

Sima had invited Soheil's sisters for tea when they visited. He was surprised by Mehri and Nadereh's reaction; they had remained mostly quiet during the tea, exchanging meaningful glances with each other every time Sima turned her face away, or went to the kitchen to get a fresh cup of tea. That was the first time he had seen his sisters so quiet, very much unlike the talkative and teasing Mehri and Nadereh he'd known all his life. Soheil couldn't understand what was happening until they left Sima's house. That was when their pointed questions started pouring out: "How long have you known each other? Do all your women friends show their hair when you visit? No scarf? Why does she smoke?" It was only then that Soheil realized his sisters found Sima and her informal manners odd. They had never talked to a man so openly, so comfortably, back in their village, and Sima's familiarity with Soheil looked suspicious

Listening to his sisters, it dawned on Soheil how much he'd changed during his time in Tehran. He felt he had jumped light years ahead of his family, no longer holding their beliefs or living his life according to their rules of propriety; he had women colleagues and friends, and sometimes they went out for lunch or dinner. He had to make sure Jasmin understood his friendship with women co-workers, or college friends. There was nothing illicit, but Jasmin could easily misread their friendly gestures, their laughter, and the comfort they obviously enjoyed the way his sisters had.

Soheil was a different man now, and he would help Jasmin to become a different woman.

He believed that a part-time job, though not at all a priority, would be good for Jasmin. He knew she'd be naturally more satisfied taking care of their children. To be a mother. No, he didn't want Jasmin to have to compete with men, to wonder why her salary was lower than theirs when she was actually more competent. That was only normal. Men provide for their families and they should be in charge. He didn't agree with those women who pushed for radical change, for better jobs and higher salaries—before society was ready. For Soheil, women's push for change only backfired, making everything worse. While ruminating about these issues, Soheil had fleeting flashbacks to the women professors he had in college, the woman dentist he visited regularly, or his women colleagues who complained privately about their lower salaries or limited opportunities. But the contradictions lost color as swiftly as they occurred to him.

Soheil knew Jasmin enjoyed a comfortable life and that no worries about money had ever occupied her mind, but he was concerned about his financial means. If he didn't make enough money, it would be particularly difficult for her; she'd lose respect for him. Imagine moving from their big home and garden to his two-bedroom apartment with no yard, not even a terrace or a balcony for fresh air. What was she going to do in a two-bedroom apartment, he asked himself?

Soheil tried to figure out the smallest details. He wanted to start right, to make their life as smooth as possible. That was his responsibility as the head of their small household. He wasn't sure how to figure out childcare if she took a part-time job, because his salary wasn't enough to pay for private daycare. He finally decided all would be well; Jasmin would take care of their babies the first few years and then they'd share the responsibility. He might even take the kids to work sometime when they were a bit older. But in the end, he knew Jasmin would love to stay at home with her children.

§

Hearing a quiet knock on his door, Soheil wondered who it could be at such an early hour of the morning when everybody was waking up or getting the children ready for school. It must be somebody on the floor, Soheil thought to himself. Cautiously opening the door a crack, he saw Amir, the next-door neighbor who lived on the same floor with his wife and one son. Amir's worried look alarmed him.

"Is everything all right?" Soheil asked immediately.

145

"Have you heard the news?" Amir asked almost inaudibly, unable to hide his worry.

"What news?"

Soheil had spent the past few nights wrapping up the report his boss wanted, so he could present it at his upcoming meeting. The night before, he had gone to bed exhausted but content because he had finally managed to finish the project; only a few changes were needed, and he could take care of them in the morning before going to work. The only thing on his mind was the report; the sooner he finished it, the earlier he could take off for his village.

"The earthquake!" Amir muttered.

"What earthquake?"

Soheil felt impatient to go back to his report. He hadn't turned on the radio, as usual, going instead to his small desk to wrap up his report.

"In Roodbar. In Manjil," Amir said haltingly.

Soheil stood by his door, and stared at Amir in utter disbelief. Finally, he heard his own voice, "Manjil?"

"I didn't want to give you the news, but my wife told me we should check on you," Amir said shyly, uncertain what to say next.

Running to the radio, Soheil turned it on to the highest volume, as though that way it would disseminate more accurate information. Simultaneously he reached for his television. All of a sudden, images of the earthquake filled the room. He tried to maintain his calm by pushing away disturbing thoughts. Sitting on the floor, he tried to concentrate on the names of the places, cities and villages. Years later, Soheil still remembered the first words he heard on the radio: *"widespread damage, ... mountain villages, blocked roads, ... extensive landslides, collapsed houses ..."*

He found out the earthquake had happened in the middle of the night, but why had nobody called him? Holding his head in his two big hands, he felt his heart was going to burst out of his chest. He ran for the phone and called his parents. His sisters. His aunts. He heard only the operator's voice: "All lines are currently disconnected."

Peeking into Soheil's apartment, Amir's wife silently brought him a cup of morning tea sweetened with sugar, watching him with much worry in her eyes.

"God bless you, I am sure your family is fine," she said, clearly not believing her own false assurance.

"Have faith in God. Drink your tea; it's freshly brewed," she said consolingly.

Soheil did have faith in God, but he also feared God's wrath.

§

At first, Soheil could not believe Jasmin's death; he kept waiting for her to come back, imagining her walking in her father's orchard, hiding behind a tree, trimming honeysuckle bushes, picking a few oranges, watering the ever growing jasmine that had almost turned into a climbing tree. He remembered her green eyes, the light brown lock of hair showing from her scarf, slightly covering her pronounced forehead. In his dreams and waking hours, he talked to her about the issues they never had a chance to discuss in their real life. The only time they had together was devoted to loving each other, admiring one another, wanting to be together. Their childhood had brought them together and planted the seeds of a lifelong love; their distance had guaranteed peace and harmony, longing and desire.

He wanted to show Jasmin's family that he was a faithful man, that he'd remain loyal to her in life and in death. If her young body was buried in the village's cemetery, her memory was still alive, calling him to her at all times. He searched for her beautiful green eyes in the crowded streets, knowing too well that nobody else had those eyes. Only one in a few generations was born with that deep green color, and only in that part of the world. And now those eyes were closed forever. But for him, they remained playfully alive, following him cautiously in all he did. He'd raise his head in the middle of a meeting to see her watching him from behind the glass door, silently laughing. He was so used to looking up and spotting her watching him that he'd turned it into a playful game. Anytime he got tired or bored, he'd look down for a few seconds, knowing that she'd be waiting for him in a corner, seeking his gaze, eager for eye contact. For a secret smile. His heart sang every time he caught a glimpse of her; that was their clandestine affair in front of everybody, friend or stranger, a co-worker or his boss, and nobody suspected her presence. Taking notes at the meetings, he saw her hands moving swiftly down his notepad, jotting carefully, the way she had always taken notes at school. He always relied on her notes, so meticulous, never missing the slightest details. His desire to have Jasmin by his side had never been so strong.

The more that memories haunted him, the lonelier he became. Every time he dared to seriously consider the idea that Jasmin was gone forever, that she would never join him for the life they had so painstakingly planned, he suffered immeasurable agony. Soheil's eagerness for life, for making friends, had left him. Instead an immense sense of loneliness had engulfed him.

Walking aimlessly in the streets, he would avoid Tehran's Grand Bazaar where he and his sisters had bought the wedding ring.

§

"You still love your first wife," Pari told Soheil in her own reserved tone.

Soheil wondered why everybody tried to avoid mentioning Jasmin's name. Was it Jasmin or the memory of the devastation they were trying to escape? Everybody was affected by the earthquake; forty thousand people had perished. Thousands became homeless overnight, and nobody wanted to mention Jasmin's name. For Soheil, Jasmin's name had become part of his daily prayer. He woke up with her name and went to bed with it, promising her to always remain faithful to their love. In his mind and heart, they were married. Like real husbands and wives.

"Of course, I still love Jasmin," he had replied sharply.

Intent on not lying about his true feelings, Soheil saw no reason to bury Jasmin's memory, to wipe her out of his past as if she never existed. Jasmin was his wife since they were six years old, becoming an even stronger presence since the earthquake. She was the solace he sought, the phantom that calmed him.

Turning to Pari but avoiding her eyes, Soheil tried to sound rational and calm. "We loved each other. We never fought. We didn't separate or divorce. God took her away from me."

And he silently admitted to himself that those would always remain the sweetest days of his life.

Soheil couldn't understand why Pari did not want any trace of Jasmin in his life, why she and her family were concerned about his love of a dead woman.

Believing he was correct in keeping alive Jasmin's memory, he lost his momentary calm, and asked Pari bluntly, "Wouldn't any woman want to be loved by her husband after her untimely death?"

Soheil was too deep in his own thoughts to notice Pari's pained expression. No smile appeared on Pari's face, no understanding gesture.

As if conversing with himself out loud, Soheil pushed his point further.

"Can't one love two people at the same time?" He presumed that he had come up with the most clever question, a question that would settle everything.

Soheil expected Pari to show sympathy; she was a distant cousin, living in the same village, surviving the earthquake. Her family had suffered immensely, losing her grandparents when their house collapsed. "She'd understand the enormity of my experience, the pain I have endured," Soheil had told himself. But instead of sympathizing with him, it was Pari who demanded understanding and acquiescence, and who set the new terms. No, she did not want to be a second wife, to be held up to Jasmin, to a childish memory.

§

But it wasn't only Pari and her family who expected Soheil to leave his past behind. He felt everybody was plotting against him. Only a year after the earthquake, Ziba had gathered a list of suitable wives for her son. His sisters showed their concern by keeping up with him in spite of their own busy family lives. He felt his friends and colleagues were losing their trust in him. It was as if he were viewed as an irresponsible man, incapable of leading a healthy, normal life. As the consoling words about his loss ended with time, keen questions and pointed comments about how to properly live started. The earthquake had taken not only Jasmin but also a part of him. And now everybody was intent on burying even his memories.

Even Sima had confronted him, pushing him to choose between Pari and Jasmin, between the living and the dead. "No woman wants to compete with a phantom."

Hurt by her comment, Soheil had responded. "But Jasmin is real. Not a phantom."

"She *was* real in your youth but she is a dream now. Perhaps a nightmare. You can't bury yourself in the past. Give Pari a chance to make a life with you. Alone. Not with a ghost between the two of you."

He didn't know how to protect himself against unsolicited advice about how to go on with his life as though nothing had happened. He missed his old, confident self. Drifting in and out of social circles, he was no longer in tune with his old friends. Nothing felt right anymore. Soheil went through life's motions, his tall, strong body just carrying his lost soul, his heavy weight.

He was now a thirty-year old single man, obviously unable to start his own family. Reluctant to let go of the past. Soheil had become an uncomfortable presence in friendly gatherings.

After four years of grieving, life was no longer the same. The earthquake had become a distant memory for most. Everybody was busy living their lives, starting families, raising children, buying homes, rebuilding destroyed houses. The knowledge that he was the only unmarried man among his colleagues and friends was painstakingly disturbing. He no longer belonged to the same group of friends who earlier had promised to invite him and Jasmin for an evening tea or a Friday dinner. Nobody seemed to know what to do with a single man his age. He was too old to remain single or to befriend younger, unmarried men. He belonged nowhere.

Staying unmarried had become a stigma that he carried indignantly. Soheil had to prove that he was a trustworthy man, as dependable as before: an honorable man who stood strong in the face of life's calamities, big or small.

It was time to start again. Convincing himself to trust women's instincts in such matters as marriage and family, Soheil finally obliged Pari. He stopped calling on Jasmin's family when he visited his village. He had become like their son: they had grieved together and consoled one another. But no more. He stopped going to the cemetery with a bouquet of lilies-of-the-valley, the tiny heavenly scented flowers he and Jasmin had picked in the valley as children. Jasmin had to become part of his past, buried a second time, if Soheil wanted to be taken seriously. In years to come, he'd tell his children about the earthquake, but not about his first love.

Errand Boy

HAMID WAS DRIVING his brand-new car, enjoying the smooth ride in spite of the frenetic traffic that was getting more congested as he neared the city. His gated suburban home shielded him from the city's non-stop noise, air pollution, and swarms of people always in motion. He didn't like to go to Tehran; once a week to take care of his business was more than enough.

He was only vaguely familiar with the general area he was driving to, and didn't know exactly where the house was located. He figured he'd ask once he got closer to his destination. There were many new suburbs and neighborhood expansions, but he had missed most of that construction since moving to the outskirts of the city. The revolution brought his successful import business to a halt by changing the rules. The sanctions only exacerbated the already volatile situation. Disturbed by the turn of the events, he wanted no part of what was happening in the country. His home became his cell from where he managed his business affairs. It took him about ten years to release himself from his self-imposed solitary confinement.

How ugly these constructions are, Hamid thought as he drove past the newly built gray rectangular apartment blocks. No design, no artistic or creative architecture to soothe the eye. Purely functional and utterly unsightly. Although they were only a few years old, the buildings already looked dilapidated. He couldn't get over the fact that people proudly saved for years to buy one of these hideous apartments. He could see from a distance that some didn't even have proper curtains or shades, hanging plain sheets over the windows instead. Only a few had installed window air conditioners.

We have built magnificent monuments lasting for centuries, surviving even the Mongol attacks, and now look at these houses, Hamid growled to himself. They look worse than our graveyards. A cemetery for the living. When he was a child, his parents had lived in a dilapidated house shared with other families. Perhaps that explained his intense dislike of the dreary buildings.

None of the streets had familiar names. He wondered who had come up with such names. In his youth, there was Eisenhower Avenue, Churchill Boulevard, Roosevelt Avenue and Kennedy Square. Nowadays, streets were names to commemorate war martyrs, prominent figures such as Shahid Beheshti, or religious or political notions like Freedom Street and Equality Square.

Believing he'd probably gone too far, he lowered his window at the red light and asked the taxi driver in the next lane where Asgari Street was. The taxi driver had just enough time to point back before the light turned green. Making an illegal U-turn, Hamid swore at other drivers for not letting him easily complete his turn. He brought traffic to an abrupt halt. "Can't they see I'm only making a U-turn?" he grumbled.

Driving a couple blocks in the opposite direction, he felt awfully confused. He considered parking his car and going into one of the shops to get better directions. Park here? In this neighborhood? Not a good idea, he thought to himself. I shouldn't have driven this car.

Finally he decided that since the car had the latest alarm system, nobody could get close to it without the alarm going off and making an earsplitting noise. Even the neighborhood stray cats were scared of his car; if they happened to jump on it, the alarm would scare them away immediately.

Hamid double-parked, making sure his doors were locked before running into the closest store. He walked up to the cashier and loudly asked where Asgari Street was. A few customers in line stared at him curiously while others started giving directions simultaneously.

He wasn't far from the street he was looking for, he was told.

Driving another block and a half, he finally spotted Asgari Street. Turning right, he went all the way to the Melli Alley, where he couldn't go any further.

"Why didn't I come by cab?" Hamid grumbled again. "Anything can happen in this neighborhood." Parking the car reluctantly, he examined the façades of the stores and houses. Cautiously scanning passersby, he did not see a single friendly face. Buttoning up his coat, he started walking up the alley. He knew he was looking for the fifth house on the right, with a gray wooden door. He walked slowly on the left side of the alley to get a good view of the building before ringing the doorbell.

There it was: House 67, Melli Alley. Checking the number a second time, he kept walking without pause, without ringing the doorbell. His palms sweated in spite of the cool autumn weather. He had imagined all sorts of houses, but nothing like this. It looked shoddier than he expected.

Garbage was strewn in the street. Hungry, emaciated cats searched the scattered trash for food. A group of children played soccer with a half-deflated plastic ball; they paused for a moment to look at Hamid, and then started playing again. His eleven-year-old son, Kamran, had three soccer balls back home, just left in the yard.

The odor of the garbage was sickening. Hamid knew poverty, but his adult life had pleasantly shielded him against such wretchedness. He was now a wealthy man, respected by friends and relatives. He had earned his position in life through sheer business acumen. As a high school dropout, he had done a marvelous job providing for his parents when they were at their lowest. When his father could no longer work, Hamid had become the family breadwinner at sixteen.

Turning on his heel, he reluctantly returned to house 67 and cautiously pushed the side of his thumb on the doorbell, trying to minimize contact between his hand and the wall. He had promised his son, Farhad, that he would visit him Monday afternoon. He was late.

§

"Wow, what are these pastries for? Are we having company?" Farhad's sister Mina asked joyfully while reaching into the box to pick one. They never bought Danish.

"Yes, we are having a guest," Farhad said gently. "Father is coming for a visit."

Putting the roll carefully back in the box, Mina looked at Farhad questioningly.

"When?"

"This afternoon. He promised to come."

"Why? Have you been talking to him? Without telling me?" Mina felt hot, her heart suddenly racing.

"Yes." A long pause followed Farhad's confession. "I have been visiting him at his office."

"But why?"

"I wanted to see him." Farhad was trying to sound casual.

"Why didn't you tell me?"

"I knew you wouldn't agree," he said gently. Looking straight at Mina, he added, "And I didn't know how to tell you. I didn't want to upset you."

"Why did you want to see him?"

"I don't know. Perhaps to make amends?"

"You think you can find the father we never had?"

After his divorce, Hamid kept the children, although he could not take care of them alone. For years he sent them to different family members. When his elderly mother finally told him she couldn't look after the children all the time, he placed them with his sister who already had three of her own. A few months later, an old widowed aunt took them in for some time. Mina and Farhad hated each new place. Hamid didn't think he'd done anything wrong because the law gave him the right to custody.

Mina and Farhad learned to take care of their sickly grandmother and then the widowed aunt. They babysat for another aunt's little children. From a very young age, they learned what it means to be old, fragile, and forgetful. They also learned to live with deprivation, eating only bread and cheese day after day. Hamid never considered the option of having them live with their mother Feri and her family. They would have been more than happy to have the children. He believed there was a reason for the centuries old law to give custody to fathers, no matter how devastated mothers felt. No matter how miserable Farhad and Mina felt.

"I have to try," Farhad said calmly. "I owe it to myself. To us."

"He hated us. As if we were not his children," said Mina. "He has never been a father to us."

"Mina *june*, he didn't hate us. He just didn't know any better." Farhad put his hand on Mina's shoulder, trying to calm her.

"He didn't know any better? That doesn't explain or forgive anything."

"Mina, he's changed. He is not the same man we knew."

"Things have changed. We're adults. The law can no longer dictate how we should live our life. Now that mother lives with us, nobody can take her away, and father can't say a word about that."

Farhad believed that everybody needed a second chance. He owed it to himself, to his sister, perhaps to his stepbrother and sister. He was ashamed of telling people, his friends and colleagues, that yes, he has a father but they don't talk. That they never visit each other. That they have never talked to each other.

"I want our father to be with us the day you marry. So we can tell your in-laws that yes, although our parents are divorced, we love both of them and they love us," Farhad said proudly.

"All I know is that he was never a father to me. Nor to you," Mina said before going to her room.

§

Farhad had started visiting Hamid once a week at his office. At the beginning, his visits were short, talking mostly about relatives.

"I haven't seen uncle Majid for a long time? How is he doing? Has his son married?"

Hamid didn't offer much information. "Yes, he married a good woman."

Reluctant to give up, Farhad inquired about his other cousins. "I heard Nasrin is going to college. She was always very smart. She's admitted to the Tehran University. That's pretty good. Is she studying accounting?"

"So what? She'd have to marry at some point, and all that education and money will be a waste. So many girls are going to college these days only to marry later and forget all about their degrees."

Farhad wondered what else there was to talk about after all the relatives and their children were discussed? He was worried he was running out of topics. Hamid was a man of few words, but Farhad sensed there was more to him than the loud silence he hid behind. What was he scared of? What was he trying to bury? Farhad wasn't sure how to penetrate the overbearing reserve Hamid maintained, but he also felt another person was hiding there, eager to reveal his soul.

In time, Farhad felt his visits went smoother. Hamid still didn't talk much, but he looked more relaxed and seemed calmer. He was getting to know his father little by little. He found out that his father was not interested in politics, business talk, or family issues. Even as a successful man, he was not interested in talking about money. They sat in his dimly lit office and didn't turn the ceiling-lights on when evening shadows began to creep across the walls, engulfing the room in mystery.

"For some reason, I like the slow darkness that changes the shape of everything. In the dark, you can rely only on your memory to find what you want. It's only then that I feel at peace," Hamid once said.

Farhad couldn't understand his father's need for dim light, for taking solace in darkness; he felt the darkness brought them together while keeping them separate. They could see each other's figures but their facial expressions were barely visible. Their hushed voices added to the tranquil mood of the enclosed office, especially against the noisy backdrop of street life. They began to feel relief in hearing each other's voice, although they were both conscious of its fragile nature. Farhad cautiously hoped there was the possibility of connecting to the father he always wanted.

§

"Remember, we needed money when I wanted to start my own shop?" asked Farhad.

Mina remembered that well. They had contacted all their relatives and friends to borrow money so Farhad could rent a shop to start his own tailoring business. Everybody had turned down their request for a loan, believing he wouldn't be able to pay them back. But all of a sudden, the building's manager reduced the rent and Farhad was finally able to open his own place. They took that as a goodwill sign and always thanked the manager profusely.

"You know I am the only person in the building who is paying a rent lower than the others? I am not paying for the utilities either."

"Don't tell me he has been covering for you all this time!" said Mina, refusing to refer to Hamid as father.

"Without father's help, I'd be still working for other people."

"How do you know he was the one who helped?"

"Because I know!"

Mina sat quietly, barraged by her emotions. Sorting out her thoughts, she sensed anger more than anything else, but she tried to stay quiet and not to explode.

"Maybe he helped you when others refused to do so, but he hasn't changed."

"But he is a different man now," Farhad objected.

"Farhad, do whatever you want. But remember, he couldn't even see us happy."

A bitter smile covered Farhad's face. They did have a good few months with their mother Feri until their stepmother Sima discovered Feri had secretly moved in with them. It was as if Sima had spies all over town. The moment she found out about their living arrangement, the house was sold and the money conveniently deposited in the bank in Sima's name. This was the same house that Hamid had bought for his mother, the first and the last house she ever owned. To buy a house for his mother had made Hamid a proud son.

"Yes, I remember that," Farhad said sadly.

Kindly looking into his eyes, Mina murmured, "I wish I were as kindhearted as you, but I can't forgive him. For what he did to us. And to mother."

Farhad did not blame Mina. Of the two of them, she was the elder and the one who had it worse after Hamid divorced Feri. He could remember the many nights that he woke up, hearing Mina sobbing quietly in bed. As a little skinny boy, he'd lie down next to her, putting his arm around her shoulder, promising that everything would be all right.

§

It hadn't taken long for Hamid to marry Sima, the young law student who was interning at divorce court. Sima had given Hamid valuable advice for his divorce procedure, and he had found her beautiful and charming.

Mina bitterly remembered overhearing from another room the ultimatum Sima had given one night. "Either they go or I go. I can't take care of two brats in this house." And there they went, banished, out of sight, out of mind. Two little exiles.

§

"I have been thinking about my father a lot," Hamid said during one of Farhad's office visits. "You remember grandfather, don't you?"

Farhad barely remembered his grandfather. He was only seven when he passed away.

"He was fifty years old when he had me," Hamid said. "Too old to be a father. Never thought I'd be able to make a living for myself."

Farhad had never heard these stories. He didn't know that his grandfather had no faith in Hamid, the man who had become a symbol of success for the family. Sitting still in his wooden chair, Farhad was all ears. Not wanting to interrupt Hamid's train of thought, he did not move so much as a finger. Neither did he ask a question.

As a gardener, suffering from rheumatism, Hamid's father had been barely able to make a living for his family. He worked for different people who paid a pittance. He was mostly on his knees weeding, digging, and planting on hot summer days. After his rheumatism got worse, he became almost debilitated by chronic pain, losing job after job.

"God bless your grandmother. She was a kind soul; she took me to the Laleh Zar shopping district and asked every shop owner if they had a job for me." Traces of a faint smile appeared on his face. "She did the same in our own neighborhood."

Hamid had watched his mother making all sorts of promises. In the carpentry shop, she talked about how precise he was in measuring everything. In the mechanic shop, she boasted about how fast he learned everything. In the fabric store, she praised his charm, the ability to attract customers. Listening to his mother, Hamid had come to believe he had all of these talents. On the way back home on the bus, she held his hand tight in hers, and they smiled together.

"One day Mr. Cohen the fabric shop owner came to our house and took me to Mr. Mizrahi, who had a yarn shop. His sons were studying in the U.S. and he needed help running his store. That was the last day I went to school. I was fourteen."

Farhad thought about ironies, about comparisons between Hamid's life and his own. He too had quit school to make money, never going back to finish his diploma. Farhad could vividly remember his last day of school; keeping his big eyes half closed, careful not to utter a word, afraid he might break into sobbing. Feri found out only later and made Farhad promise to go to night classes. He never did.

Deep in his heart, Farhad blamed Hamid for not being able to finish high school. He could have gone to the university had he gotten his diploma.

"Did you ever regret quitting school?" Farhad asked.

"No, I didn't miss school at all." A proud smile covered Hamid's face. "What I was doing was much more interesting. I was making money! A lot of money in a very short time. I felt rich. We were no longer wretchedly poor."

Hamid learned the tricks of the trade fast. Mr. Mizrahi taught him how to treat customers, to discern real shoppers from browsers. Hamid learned what kind of yarn to order and from which countries. Switzerland and India were his favorites. He even started learning how to knit, showing the customers fancy knitting patterns in foreign journals. Taking knitting journals home, his mother and sisters spent hours figuring out different patterns. He took their samples to the shop to show the customers. He could answer all of their questions.

"I learned I could make a living buying and selling yarn. I was only sixteen and I was supporting my family, giving my mother all the money I made. She was so proud of me."

Farhad couldn't imagine his father learning to knit. *A man knitting?* he would certainly scoff.

"Father couldn't believe I was making money, real money, supporting the entire family. For the first time we were eating good food. Meat and fruit. A few years later, I bought your grandmother the first house she ever owned."

Hamid revealed little by little, usually just a bit before nine o'clock, when Farhad had to leave to catch the last bus. Was Hamid trying to prolong their Wednesday visits? Did he want to make sure there wasn't enough time to reveal too much so that Farhad would be back next week for more? Farhad had no idea. But he knew one thing: Hamid had started to look forward to seeing his son. The quiet man who at first barely smiled now couldn't hide his pleasure at seeing Farhad. He had even started coming down to the lobby to greet him personally. That was good progress, Farhad thought to himself. Farhad began to look forward to Wednesdays, to hear more about Hamid's past.

§

"You know, I haven't told mother that you see him," Mina said quietly.

"That's all right. Let's keep it between us for now. I don't want her to get upset or worried," Farhad said after a long silence.

Believing that Farhad would stop seeing Hamid sooner or later, Mina agreed that Feri shouldn't know anything about Farhad's visits.

Mina knew how humiliated and ashamed Feri had felt after the divorce, having to go back to her parents' house, unable to support herself. For months, she had avoided her relatives, embarrassed to show her face in family gatherings. She had become not only an object of pity but also an easy target for men who wanted to have a second wife or perhaps an easy affair. The neighborhood grocer and baker had already shown much indiscreet interest, recommending marriage before she lost her marketability, each claiming to be kind husbands, unlike some men. Feri had started shopping further south in the neighborhood where people did not know her as a divorced woman, and avoided casual conversations with people.

Hamid had become the only source of tension that ever existed between Mina and Farhad. Mina felt insecure; she was acutely conscious of the nights Farhad came home late. Noticing Farhad's regular absence for Wednesday dinners, Feri had also shown her own concern.

"Is he seeing somebody?" Feri would ask anxiously. "Perhaps a girl? They shouldn't be in the streets this late. Or even go to a restaurant. Young people get into all sorts of trouble these days. The morality police will pick them up; there is no telling what might happen to them if they get arrested."

"No, Feri *june*. Don't worry. He hasn't mentioned any girls. He'd tell us if he was dating. He's just working late. They probably have a lot of orders."

Mina felt frustrated; living together with Farhad and their mother obviously could not last forever, but she did not want to think anything would disturb the peace and quiet they had gained after years of insecurity. What the law, their father, and his relatives had prevented from happening had finally changed by the time they came of age. Mina loved their living arrangement. She felt victorious to have overcome the legal cruelty that gave custody to the father, even to a neglectful father like Hamid. No, she didn't want to change a thing. There were times she thought that even if Farhad decided to marry at some point, she would never marry. She would stay with Feri. She would remain her daughter and lifelong companion.

Envisioning the image of mother and daughter together brought a sweet smile to her face. And to her heart.

§

"I never forget the day I saw Raha," Hamid casually said one day.

Farhad could hardly contain his curiosity. Who? Who was this girl he had never heard about?

"She is still with me." Chuckling to himself, he added softly, "In my arms." He then paused momentarily to see Farhad's reaction. Noticing the surprised look on his face, Hamid smiled gently and said, "Son, I mean in my dreams. I am still embracing my girl in my dreams. And some days in complete wakefulness, I walk with her in the park, sitting on a bench shielded by a big weeping willow tree, holding her soft, delicate hand in mine."

Astonished by Hamid's frankness, it dawned on Farhad that there was another woman in his father's life. He felt curious about his own feelings when he realized a smile was forming on his lips.

"She came to the store with her mother one day. Fair face, light brown eyes, black hair flowing down her shoulders like a waterfall. It was obvious they were important customers because Mr. Mizrahi came out of his office immediately to greet them personally. I helped him bring out the fancy yarn he kept in his backroom for special customers."

Farhad felt a pang of jealousy; he had never met anybody important in his life, let alone a girl from a wealthy family with hair flowing over her shoulders. By the time Farhad came to understand anything, all the girls had to cover their hair in a scarf, if not a black chador. The revolutionary regime demanded women's bodies be completely covered.

Thank goodness we can at least see women's faces, Farhad thought to himself. He considered his father's generation lucky, for they could date girls, especially if they went to the university. Farhad had never seen flowing hair, except Mina's, his mother's, and a few relatives'. His grandmother always covered her unruly gray hair with a scarf; she had never completely changed her ways before or after the revolution. Hamid's quiet voice brought Farhad back to the room, to his immediate surroundings.

"Mr. Mizrahi ordered saffron pistachio ice cream for them. As they were exchanging pleasantries, the girl started playing with the yarn, mixing and matching different colors and textures without a word. Not a sound from her."

Hamid watched the girl from the corner of his eyes. She touched the soft fuzzy threads, pushing her long, shapely fingers through the yarn balls. But she wasn't only playing; she picked different textures and sizes. Hamid put more colorful yarn in front of her, careful not to attract any attention. He could feel the heat of her body, the electricity of her hair. Her ice cream melted in front of her while she played with the yarn.

"I was standing by the counter. Noiselessly. I saw her tugging at her mother's dress as she pointed at her creation. There it was: A yarn girl! She had a figure of a girl made out of yarn, holding an orange yarn purse in her hand. Wearing orange yarn shoes. Her eyes were beaming with delight. Her face, the shape of her hand, and that of her long, slender fingers never left me. Not to this day."

That was the first day Hamid saw Raha, but not the last. He learned where the mother and daughter lived because he delivered their packages. He was not surprised when he saw they had the biggest and nicest house in Mr. Mizrahi's neighborhood.

§

"Did you ever talk to her?" Farhad asked his father sympathetically.

"Never." A painful expression engulfed Hamid.

Farhad wished that his father had more sense than to fall in love with a girl from a wealthy family.

"I couldn't wait to deliver yarn to the Kazemi's house. I even volunteered to deliver new kinds we received."

Hamid would run half the way to the Kazemi's, but the moment he rang the doorbell, his mouth would dry up and he'd lose his speech like a kid. The maid took the packages from him and led him to the kitchen.

"They were a kind family, never letting me leave their home without eating something, maybe a cup of tea with cookies, some cool drink, or occasionally an ice cream. Their kitchen was as big as our entire little apartment, with chairs and a round table. I had never seen a round table. My mother's kitchen was a burner she had in a corner."

For Farhad it was clear his father didn't have any consciousness of Raha's feelings, or what she might have actually thought about him. He had seen Mina fuming with anger when uncouth men expressed interest in her. Apparently, the possibility that Raha could despise Hamid, feel utterly disgusted, or even humiliated if she ever found out that an errand boy was interested in her, totally escaped Hamid. Worse, it seemed it had never occurred to Hamid that the Kazemis would be appalled by a nobody, clerk boy, daring to even look at their daughter. None of that mattered to Hamid, for all he could think of was his blind love for Raha.

The son who had worked late into the night at the yarn shop was now going to bed early to think about Raha. He left home in the morning to be at her house to escort her to school. He did not make himself visible, always walking behind her, within a reasonable distance to keep an eye on her. He found himself mesmerized by the way her hair changed color in the afternoon glow compared to the morning sun, reflecting a thousand shades of black and brown. He even enjoyed the trembling in his heart. It was a sensation he had never experienced before.

§

One day at the yarn shop, Hamid was seized by the desire to hear Raha's voice. He had heard it in his dreams time and again. Looking through Mr. Mizrahi's notebook, he easily found the Kazemis' phone number. One look and the number became part of his memory. The six numbers became his lucky mantra, and he repeated them like a love song, until the day he made his first phone call. And the days after that when he could no longer stay away from the phone.

The phone became another obsession, offering an opportunity for hearing Raha's voice. He didn't wonder why it was always Raha's mother, sister, or brother who answered the phone. Each time absolute silence greeted the family. Again, it didn't occur to him that the Kazemis were alarmed by these mysterious phone calls. Neither did he suspect why Raha no longer walked to school. Or why she was chauffeured around all the time, never left alone anymore. Suddenly, Raha was no longer anywhere to be seen. She completely disappeared, not even chauffeured in the backseat of her father's Peugeot.

Unbeknownst to Hamid, the family had decided to send Raha to her aunt in Stockholm for summer vacation. To get her away from the stalker who called day and night. Unable to find out who was after their fourteen-year-old daughter, the family had chosen the safest route. Remove Raha from her immediate surroundings for a time.

Desperate to see her, Hamid became a self-designated guard, keeping an eye on the Kazemis' house, standing in a corner waiting for the door to open to get a glimpse of his love. At nights he walked the streets aimlessly, like a lost soul, in a state of delirium, devastated by the prospect of never seeing Raha again.

Darkness descended not only on Hamid, but also on his parents. He plunged into a deep melancholy; the boy turned into man too early for his own sake was fired for missing work. Hamid, the son who had only recently made his father proud by the money he made, turned into a source of anxiety. His family suffered as their brief period of financial relief came to an end.

§

"How could they do this to me?" Hamid asked despairingly, even after so many years. "I didn't mean any harm. I was just a clerk boy who opened and closed the store. An errand boy. But I was in love." Reflecting on his feelings, on the agony he was subjected to, Hamid continued, "Now that I am much older, I think maybe it was just youthful infatuation. Who knows? Whatever it was, it ruined my life."

Farhad was surprised to see how quickly Hamid's grave tone changed into a jovial voice as he continued, "But in my dreams, I was with her and she was with me. All the time. We walked together, hand in hand. I protected her from all evil, from all the preying eyes. I was her guardian. I felt alive for the first time in my life."

Farhad didn't need to prod Hamid. He talked as if he had forgotten Farhad was listening.

§

Happy to find an open seat on the bus, Farhad sank down, leaning his head against the rattling window, closing his eyes. He had a long ride and wanted to shut off the outside world, its people, noise, troubles, and feelings. He felt unsettled by the stories Hamid had so frankly shared with him and needed time to retreat into his own world.

Sorry, that's how he felt for his father. The ambiguous feeling he initially had was giving way to sad compassion. The all-powerful wealthy father who had ruined his childhood was slowly changing into a helpless errand boy, and Farhad wasn't completely ready for that image. He'd reached a point where he needed to talk too.

§

"Mother and father's marriage was arranged," Farhad told Mina when Feri was still at work.

"They married in 1965; a lot of marriages were arranged in those days. That's no big deal," Mina said, pretending indifference.

"Yes, but father was forced to marry mother."

"What do you mean? Nobody can force a man to marry," she snapped back. "Plus, if he was forced to marry, I am sure mother didn't have a say either."

"Maybe mother didn't have a say, but at least she wasn't in love with someone else."

"He loved another woman before marrying mother?" Mina asked curiously.

"While he married mother."

"Did he have another wife?"

Farhad looked at Mina in bafflement, wondering how she reached that conclusion. Seeing her so serious, he started laughing. He had anticipated all kinds of reactions from Mina, but not a humorous spin on the unhappy story of Hamid's life. He appreciated the comic relief, though; it helped him unburden himself from the pain that still seemed to be alive in Hamid.

Seeing him laughing at her, Mina turned to him and said admonishingly, "Farhad, tell me what you know. You know I don't like guessing games."

"Well, if you want to hear the whole story, we need two big glasses of tea."

Mina placed the tea on the small coffee table. "Be careful, they are really hot." As she sat down on the couch, she took off her shoes, folding her legs under her in order to face Farhad. "Now tell me. No jokes. No mysteries."

"Do you remember Grandpa?"

Mina remembered. He scared her. She tried to stay as close to her mother as possible when they visited. Kissing her on the forehead, he held her firmly in his arms and sat her down by himself. She couldn't wait to run to Feri, discreetly testing his big tight grip every couple minutes to see if the old man had loosened his hold. She felt like a hunted bird with her wings tied together.

"Yes, I remember him. He had such an angry frown, with his thick arched eyebrows, never a smile," Mina said in a gloomy way. "I learned one thing from him—don't ever hug little girls. They're afraid of stern wrinkly people. And they don't want to be touched or held so tightly."

"Grandpa chose Feri for father."

"A lot of people chose their own wife by then. How come our father didn't choose his own? Farhad, what has he been telling you? That he was forced to marry mother? That she was the reason for his misery? That she was never good enough for him?"

"No, he doesn't blame mother. He knows he's the one who has wronged her."

"Really?" Mina said vindictively. "That's a little too late, isn't it?"

"At least he is truthful," said Farhad.

"Excuse me, but that's the least he could say. So now we are supposed to sympathize with him?"

As far as Mina was concerned Hamid did everything he could to prevent Feri from living with them. He ruined their childhood.

Putting his hands over his face, Farhad gently rubbed his eyes, keeping them closed for a few seconds. "You're not letting me finish the story," Farhad finally said reproachfully.

"No, I am not. What do I need his story for? He is telling you all this to absolve himself. He got rid of Mother and us to jump into the arms of a much younger woman, an intern for heaven's sake. This is the truth, not the nonsense he's been telling you."

"I am not disagreeing with you. But I think it's important to hear his side too," Farhad said quietly. He reached for his tea when he realized that neither of them had touched their glasses.

"Would you like fig preserve with your tea?" he asked, trying to sound conciliatory.

"No…yes…sure," Mina said absentmindedly.

"I'll go and get it. You stay here."

Farhad collected the tea glasses and calmly walked to the kitchen.

"I'll get us some hot tea too."

Taking his time in the kitchen, Farhad rinsed the glasses, poured boiling water in them, and swished it around, letting the glass absorb the heat of the water. Emptying the water, he mixed the tea with more boiling water. He knew Mina liked her tea very strong and boiling hot. Putting the two glasses and the fig preserve on a tray, he took it to the living room where Mina was sitting, still seething in anger, her lips pressed as if she was scared her thoughts might fly out of her mouth involuntarily. Putting the tray on the coffee table, Farhad said, "Now drink your tea before it gets cold again, and don't interrupt me till I finish my story." Pausing for a second, he added, "I mean his version of the story."

Mina leaned back, grabbing a pillow and folding it over her chest. Her whole body felt tense; she could feel a headache encroaching.

"He married mother because he was ashamed of telling his parents he was in love. The girl he loved was from a rich family, and he was only an errand boy. A school dropout with no prospects. Or at least that's what everybody thought at the time. He was crazy about that girl." Pausing for a moment, Farhad added somberly, "Who knows? Perhaps he had completely lost his mind. At least for some time."

"Obviously, he never got it back," Mina said crossly, satisfied with her biting comment.

Catching Farhad's reproachful look, she asked, "A clerk in a store? I thought he was always rich."

"So much we don't know about our father," Farhad responded.

"It's not our fault."

Ignoring Mina's comment, he continued. "He lost his job and started roaming the streets in search of his love."

Mina stared at Farhad silently.

"Grandpa thought marriage would solve Father's problem and would send him back to work to make money again. It would teach him to be a man."

Mina held the tea in her hand with a firmer grip.

"I feel sorry for him, Mina. The more he talks to me the more I realize how miserable he has been."

Mina got up and turned on the lamp. She needed light. Walking from room to room, she tried to keep her anger to herself. It was clear Farhad sympathized with Hamid. She didn't want to utter an unwise word or make an undiplomatic comment. She had said enough. The last thing she wanted was to hurt Farhad. They were one voice, one heart, bearing the same kind of pain all their life.

"Grandpa found a wife for Father in no time. He took him to meet the girl and her family only after everything was finalized. The two families had agreed on everything: the dowry, the number of guests. Even the wedding date was set, but nobody had guessed that the groom was desperately in love with another girl."

"Farhad *june*, sorry," Mina could no longer keep quiet, "but I just don't get it. How come he didn't tell anyone? Not even Grandma? She would have understood. How come he didn't object?"

"But he did! He refused to visit Mother and her parents. He stayed away till the wedding night, but he was afraid of saying anything openly. But our grandfather was a clever man. Sensing his son's reluctance, he had recruited the entire family to encourage, persuade, cajole, or chastise him. Whatever it took. Everybody had teamed up against him, believing his only cure was marriage.

"His uncle Amir told him," Farhad continued, "'We have gone to their house to ask for this girl's hand. They have accepted our conditions, and now you don't even go to their house to pay respect? This is dishonorable. You don't understand what's in your best interest. In this family, a son doesn't disrespect his father like that.'"

"I remember him. I never liked him," Mina said.

"His grandmother tried to console him, telling him that he'd learn to love his bride. That she was a good girl from a good family. That love will come with time. With patience and understanding.

"His Aunt Fatima told him straight that they couldn't back off any more. If they did, everybody would think there was something wrong with the girl. 'If you don't marry her,' she said, 'you have ruined her reputation. Disrespected her family. She won't be able to hold her head high up among family and friends or in the neighborhood. Nobody will ask for her hand; you can't shame her like that.'

"Mr. Cohen pulled him aside to tell him, 'You can't ridicule your elderly father like that, making him the joke of the neighborhood.'

"Even the shop owners in the neighborhood were involved. The grocer had his own advice. 'It's no big deal son, if she doesn't please you, you can always marry a second wife. See, I have two wives, ten children, and I am planning to get another one soon. I will give her a dowry, too. Women are good for you. You won't lose anything. Marry her before you're too old.' The grocer had told him with a big smile, showing his missing teeth."

As if talking to himself, Farhad went on, "Father told me he did not look at Feri's face even on the wedding day, keeping his eyes glued to the carpet. He went through the motions, like a robot, a good son who obeyed his father unquestioningly.

"And the wedding happened on the scheduled day with fifty-five guests. Some of the store owners of the neighborhood were also invited, out of respect for their valuable advice."

Mina sat in silence as Farhad finished his story.

"I am lucky nobody can tell me who to marry," Farhad's sighed with relief.

§

"But what about mother?" Farhad heard himself asking. This was the first time he had made a reference to Feri in front of Hamid. "What did she feel in all this?"

"I knew you'd ask that question." After a long pause, he answered, "Son, it was an unfortunate match for both of us. Perhaps more so for your mother. She became the target of my anger, the visible sign of my defeat. The longer we lived together, the more bitter I became."

Even in the encroaching evening shadows, Farhad could sense Hamid's frustration, as if Feri had been the only source of his misery.

"I plunged into a deep depression. Imagine! Forced to marry. Compelled to live with a girl I had no interest in, especially after I'd tasted love, felt the excitement, the energy it gives you. Your mother was everything I didn't want."

Farhad didn't want to hear the whole of the naked truth his father was telling him, but Hamid seemed haunted by his memories. It felt as though he still loathed Feri. And for no good reason. As far as Farhad was concerned, Feri was a helpless victim. He felt hurt by his father's harsh words, by his inconsiderate need to share his pain. It was as if Feri had not suffered, as if Farhad's childhood and life opportunities had not been ruined.

"What saved me was work." Hamid continued. "I started working with a vengeance, this time at a different store. I stayed at work, day and night, sometimes going home only for the weekend. Work became my escape. And my folks were happy again. I was making money."

At least Feri was the cause of his success—this was the first thought that flashed through Farhad's mind. He had thought again and again to tell Feri that he was seeing Hamid, but he couldn't bring himself to do that. He knew she wouldn't show anger; she had never said a negative word about Hamid, bearing her pain and shame in silence. Farhad felt his mother would understand his need to be connected to his father, to tell his future wife and in-laws that he had a father. People cared what kind of family one came from. To be a child of divorce was shameful enough. But Feri might also see Farhad's need to visit Hamid as another betrayal. If Hamid was able to pull himself through a second marriage with a much younger woman and start a new family, Feri was marked for life. As a divorced woman, she was a damaged commodity, suitable only as a second wife or a quick affair.

Farhad couldn't bring himself to cause more pain for his mother.

§

Every time Farhad visited Hamid, he learned something about this man who had abandoned his children, refusing to see them during their most impressionable years.

All his life, Farhad had wondered why Hamid was not like other fathers, picking up his children at school, buying them nice pairs of shoes for the New Year, treating them to ice cream, or gently putting coins in the palms of their little hands to give to beggars. Farhad was getting to see the wounded boy behind his father's façade, the boy who couldn't stand up against his own father's absolute rule—the boy who had grown into a man incapable of being a father to his own children.

One day, looking him straight in the eye, Hamid had laughingly blurted, "Marriage is the worst thing in life."

"But why? You have married twice. Why do you say that?"

"Because I have been married twice."

"Aren't you happy with Sima? With your two little children?"

"I was happy when I first met Sima. I thought she understood me. I saw her as my one and only friend. Somebody I could trust." Pausing gravely, Hamid added, "I mean that's how it felt at the beginning."

"And now?"

"Son, I have no friends. None whatsoever. I have learned my lesson."

§

Hamid had driven to Farhad's home with much trepidation, planning to leave right after the first cup of tea. But all his doubts melted away after the first few minutes he got there. Farhad was welcoming, overjoyed to have him. As his son went to bring tea, Hamid surveyed the furniture in the living room. The couch looked familiar; it had come as part of Feri's dowry, and she had taken it back after the divorce. Touching its upholstery, he could almost feel the threads disintegrating. The orange flowers, a color he had detested, had faded into peach. The coffee table, another dowry piece, looked rickety and unstable but was covered with a nice cloth. Although everything spoke of the lack of means, the room was clean and inviting. It invoked a plain but pleasant sense of liveliness.

All of a sudden Hamid noticed the plants placed near the windows or away from the sun. There was beautiful ivy crawling up to the ceiling, a healthy fern in a corner away from direct light, and a jasmine plant in full bloom right by the window. Blossoming jasmine in November? he thought as he picked one of the tiny little white flowers. Its pleasing fragrance brought an immediate smile to his face. Even his father couldn't bring jasmine to flower in autumn. There were no plants in his house, Hamid reflected momentarily. Sima didn't care for houseplants or anything that crowded her space.

Hamid guessed the rest of the house wasn't furnished any better. Perhaps more plants, but certainly not much furniture, except what was absolutely necessary.

The plants added a warm touch, but was this the best his children could do? His hands felt hot and sweaty. Where was I all these years? he asked himself. How could I leave them to themselves like orphans?

Farhad had never asked for anything. Once Hamid found out Farhad and Mina had started living with Feri, he was furious, feeling cheated by his own children, even though after abandoning them he hadn't bothered to find out their whereabouts. It was his cousin who told him Farhad needed start-up money to open his own business. He didn't want to have anything to do with Feri's children, but his cousin had insisted day and night, "Farhad is a good entrepreneur, capable and business-minded. Just like you. His investment would be profitable. He needs a little help, and he'll be on his own before you know."

Hamid had listened reluctantly, and had obliged only out of respect for his cousin—even then, with the full promise of remaining anonymous. He didn't want to open a door into his past, to let the dust accumulated over a decade spill into his present and contaminate his days. As far as

Hamid was concerned, his first marriage had caused only agony and trauma. Like Feri, Farhad and Mina reminded him of his past, of his powerlessness against his father, of his weakness to escape an unwanted marriage, of his unrequited love.

Yet Hamid still felt much respect for his father, the man who had hastily married him off at nineteen. That was only the beginning of other wrongs; an entangled spiral of mistakes grew to swallow him. It had taken Hamid fifteen years to divorce Feri and cut all ties with his past, and make it as if he had no children in this world. And all that only after his father had passed away. He had never asked himself why he didn't stand up to his father. Why he didn't have the courage to divorce Feri when his father was still living. Why he still had such high esteem for his father, the man who had ruined his life.

§

Farhad walked Hamid to his car. The kids were still playing in the alley under one dim street lamp. They were louder than when he had first arrived. Farhad had informed the baker that he expected his father, and told the soccer kids that if they saw a stranger, they should treat him respectfully because it was his father coming for a visit. Nobody had touched Hamid's car. The baker came out of his shop to greet them. Now that Hamid was walking with Farhad, the kids stopped their play and gathered around them, showering Hamid with questions about his brand-new car.

He now saw them as a lively bunch.

Driving back home, Hamid no longer paid attention to the ugly apartment complexes. Neither did he dwell on the uncovered windows or single lamps hanging nakedly from the ceiling. It was only when the steering wheel kept slipping under his fingers that he realized he was sweating profusely. Slowing down, he rubbed his hands against his sweater as he watched other cars race by, leaving him behind. He drove slowly, trying to concentrate. He needed to do some thinking, sort out his feelings. Dismayed, saddened, shaken? he searched for the right word, for understanding how he felt.

Whatever I feel, he told himself, my children shouldn't be living like that. Like two orphans who don't have anybody in this world. He was impressed by how Farhad had turned out, a strong, independent, and resourceful man. They deserved better; they had proven themselves while he wallowed in his misery, taking a warped satisfaction in his victimhood.

Shame and pride had awakened his numbed feelings. Pushing on the gas pedal, he thought to himself, I can't change the past, but perhaps I can be part of their future.

If only Sima would let him.

The Marriage of the Jeweler's Son

THE PHONE WAS ringing before Hamed opened his office door. "No, not this early," he groaned to himself. Eight in the morning was too early even for a desperate mother to call.

Hamed hadn't called his parents the day before, fully conscious that if he didn't soon, they would call him. It was a losing battle; since he moved to Tehran ten years ago, they talked on the phone every day. The only time their daily contact was interrupted was when he was serving at the front during the war with Iraq and couldn't be reached most of the time.

"I should stop this. Nothing has changed since our last conversation," he angrily told himself. But no strategy had worked. If Hamed didn't phone, his mother Marhamat called. If he didn't answer, his father Rahim called back and left a long heartfelt message. He could hear Rahim's words: "Hamed, *jan*, or dear, this is your father! We haven't heard from you in a long time! Are you all right? Where are you, my son? Your mother is very worried. Why don't you call and let us know how you're doing?" He ended the message with his name, "This is Rahim, your father," as if he was signing a letter.

Over the years, Hamed had seriously considered stopping their daily contact, but hearing his parents' troubled voices on his answering machine would melt away his resistance. He couldn't bear to be a source of worry for them, but he believed there must be a limit to love. Hamed knew Rahim would do anything for him. Hadn't he bought him a nice house when he moved to Tehran for college? Who buys a home for his college-age son? Even to this day, it was Rahim who was helping his children living a life beyond their reach. But Hamed wanted to be treated like the responsible adult he was. A thirty-two-year-old married man with a two year-old son.

When the phone stopped ringing, he took a long, deep breath, and felt relieved. Entering his office, he noticed the orderly surface of his desk. All the files in their place, the day's work right in front of his chair, his favorite fountain pen lying on the folder at a perfect angle. Carefully placing his coat on the wall hanger, he walked to the window to take a peek at the autumn garden. The trees were different shades of brown, and fallen leaves covered the pathways. Feeling the cool air on his clean-shaven face, he was thankful for an office with a window.

Reluctant to start his workday, Hamed considered walking to Mrs. Davoodi's office for a morning chat. He heard her walking to her office. He could always tell who walked in the hallway by just listening to their clicking or swishing footsteps. We can talk about the mother who brought her child yesterday and decide where to send her for the best help, he thought. The poor woman was at her wit's end with her child. She believed her son's Down syndrome was her fault because she had repeatedly refused her husband's advances.

"This is my penalty. God's punishment," the mother had said tearfully. "I should have listened to my husband." Quietly backing out of the office, Hamed hoped Mrs. Davoodi could convince the woman that her son's problem had nothing to do with their sex life. Sometimes

Hamed couldn't believe what people told their social workers. This case was a good excuse to visit Mrs. Davoodi, he decided. It wouldn't look suspicious in front of all the zealots who watched every greeting or interaction between men and women at work, as if even co-workers shouldn't consult each other. After all, Mrs. Davoodi was a married woman with three children, yet she always welcomed her younger colleagues into her office.

As he picked up his file and the fountain pen to make the visit more legitimate, the harsh ring of the phone jolted him. Ready to hear his mother's worried voice, he was taken aback by a seemingly familiar and friendly voice.

"Hamed *jan*, how are you doing?" the voice asked. The next words came without the slightest pause. "You don't recognize me, do you? Is that how you keep up with your old friends?" the voice said with slight amusement.

Hamed was at a loss. The caller had a personable, deep voice, reminding him of a distant past, but he couldn't figure out who he was.

"I knew you wouldn't remember me," the voice said playfully. Do you recall Professor Taheri's classes? I always sat behind you."

The warm and booming quality of the voice all of a sudden reminded him of the tall, big-boned student who sat behind him. "Oh, Ayden? It's you, isn't it?" Hamed said triumphantly, pleased with himself for remembering the caller's name.

Happy to be recognized, Ayden started chatting about their college days, naming some professors, a few of the students, who had married whom, and how many children they had. They hadn't talked for years, and the list of things to cover was endless. But as Ayden kept talking incessantly, Hamed felt a pang of concern. Suspicion rose in his chest.

People don't call to see how their old college friends are doing for nothing. Obviously there is a reason for his call, but he isn't going to tell me before chatting away for half an hour.

Hamed was sure Ayden needed some favor, maybe a recommendation for a family member, or perhaps looking for a job for himself. He couldn't tell.

"By the way, I heard you're married, and have a little son. Is that right?" said Ayden nonchalantly, apparently knowing the answer to his question already. "I married one of my classmates," Ayden offered. "Who did you marry?"

"Well, why, I married Miss Hashemi," Hamed said haltingly. "I don't believe you know her."

"Oh, yes! Did you say your wife is getting her doctorate? Her name is ah, ..." Ayden kept throwing these personal questions and bits of information at Hamed without pause.

"Is it by any chance Moneer? You said her last name is Hashemi? Right?"

This was going beyond exchanging pleasantries, Hamed thought angrily, while slowly remembering that Ayden had always irritated him as unusually curious about other people's lives. Reluctant to conceal his displeasure at this turn in their conversation, Hamed bluntly said, "I see your inquisitiveness hasn't mellowed. But why are you asking these questions?" He was extremely reluctant to discuss his wife.

Unfazed by the harsh tone, Ayden blurted out, "I thought I should let you know, my friend, but first I had to make sure I know your wife's correct name." An ominous pause followed. Hamed tried to harness his annoyance. "I saw your wife yesterday," Ayden continued, lowering his voice to a calm.

Hamed felt suspended in mid-air. "You saw my wife?" he asked crossly.

"She was at the family court where I work."

Hamed heard the deep breath Ayden took before talking again. "She was filing for divorce," continued Ayden hesitantly, "and for the full payment of her dowry."

"What?" Hamed was stunned, doubting every word Ayden said.

"What do you mean?" he said incredulously. "My wife at family court? What kind of nonsense is that? She was at work all day yesterday. I dropped her off myself." No longer in control of his temper, Hamed felt his irritation rapidly turning into a burning anger.

"My wife would never do such a thing," he blurted. Unable to stay calm, he heard himself adding agitatedly, "We've never had any problems," as if he needed to explain his relationship to Ayden.

"My friend, I'm very sorry for giving you bad news. I understand how you feel," Ayden said sympathetically. "But I thought it my duty to let you know. I saw your wife with my own eyes."

Hamed couldn't recollect the rest of their conversation. Did they talk for a long time or hang up right after Ayden gave him the news? Months later he still couldn't remember.

§

"We are going to Tehran," Marhamat told her oldest daughter Manija, though she sounded uncertain.

"Has anything happened, *Maman*?" Manija asked worriedly. "Is Hamed all right?"

"Well, why? I guess so," Marhamat said, taking a deep, though interrupted, breath. "Hamed has met a girl."

"Wow, that's great news," Manija said excitedly. "Who is she? What's her name? I'll bet she must be beautiful."

"Why, I don't know. Hamed has never been after beauty," Marhamat said confidently, as if she could read Hamed's mind and dreams. Picking up on her mother's unvoiced concern, Manija said reassuringly, "*Maman*, if Hamed has picked a wife, you shouldn't question it."

"But, why dear, I haven't said a word," she replied inaudibly.

"He's twenty-nine years old," Manija affirmed, as if Marhamat didn't know. "It's already late. If he doesn't marry now, he never will. We should encourage him. Everybody keeps asking if Hamed is still single. People gossip. Why, he doesn't mind it now, but he'll regret it sooner or later."

Since Hamed had returned from the front, his family and relatives had kept introducing potential wives—distant cousins, daughters of friends or colleagues, sisters-in-law. Even non-relatives had made intrusive inquiries.

Shopping at the neighborhood grocery store, more than once different women had beseeched Marhamat. "Is that handsome young man your son?" they'd ask.

"Why, yes," she'd reply, feeling simultaneously proud and irritated by their impudence.

"He isn't married, is he?" The impending question always created a sense of distress and concern in Marhamat. She wished she could brush the women off by proudly saying, "Why, yes, of course, he's married." But her meek answer was, "God willing, next year. He's just returned from the war."

Hamed's news was impressive enough to spread like wildfire among relatives and neighbors, old school mates and friends. The family could relax now, put their worries to rest. The eldest son of Rahim and Marhamat was getting married.

"Finally," people said among themselves. "It was about time. It's not good for a fellow to stay single for too long."

§

When his doorbell rang, Hamed thought it must be one of the neighborhood beggars, asking for food, a glass of water, or perhaps a cup of tea. *They always ring the doorbell at the oddest hours.* Walking to his door phone in the hallway, he quietly pushed the button only to hear his mother's anxious voice, "I told you, we should have called. What if he comes home late this evening?"

Hamed couldn't believe his ears. He had talked to his parents the day before, and they didn't mention anything about traveling to Tehran. Had they driven 400 kilometers to see him without saying a word? He felt thrown off.

His father's cheerful voice contrasted with Marhamat's expressed concern. "No worries. He's always home by eight o'clock."

Rahim's confident and truthful words stung Hamed. For a moment, he felt transfixed by his door phone.

"He might be at a friend's home for dinner," said Marhamat, obviously not convinced. "He's home all right. He doesn't spend time with friends on week nights," Rahim said.

Was the truth always this hurtful? Hamed pondered before automatically pushing the open button. The fact was he would visit friends or colleagues neither on weeknights nor on weekends. All his friends were married, and to get invited to friends' houses, one had to be married, and preferably with children. At twenty-nine, Hamed was still single, barely contemplating marriage.

Watching the door clicking open before them, Marhamat and Rahim abruptly ended their conversation, looking expectantly at the half-opened door.

"Didn't I tell you he was home?" Rahim said joyfully. "Your mother was worried you may not be home."

Marhamat kissed her son, hugging him closely. "You've lost weight, sweetheart." Tenderly touching his hair, she went on, "You're not eating well?"

"No, he's as strong as ever," Rahim said while pulling his son tightly into a heartfelt embrace.

"Come on in. Why didn't you tell me you were coming?" Hamed asked as he reached for their two small bags sitting by the door. "Is everything all right?"

"Everything is better than all right, son," Rahim said excitedly. "We have come to meet the family of the girl you mentioned last night."

Stunned, Hamed almost tripped over his doorstep. "Which girl?" he asked, as if he had no recollection of what he had told them the night before.

"You've already forgotten her!" Rahim said teasingly. "The girl you've been helping with her research. You wanted us to meet her. Miss Moneer. Didn't you say her name is Moneer? A good suitable name, indeed. Who did you say her people were?" he inquired kindly, showing his excitement.

Setting their bags down in the hallway, Hamed straightened his back, turning to his father in disbelief. "I just mentioned this girl I have seen a few times, but I didn't mean ..."

Interrupting him, Rahim said joyfully, "We know how you feel. Call her family tomorrow to arrange a visit. I have left the shop to your cousin, but we can't stay for long. This is a good month for business. So many weddings! Only yesterday, I had three families at the shop. People want to buy their wedding rings; as you know, half of our sale happens this month.

§

Hamed knew his parents were anxious for him to marry. Of their four children, he was the only one still single. Even his younger brother already had a wife and a five-year-old son. Rahim blamed the war. Marhamat believed it was Hamed's move to Tehran. "He left the family at such an early age," she always reminded Rahim. "The poor boy has been on his own for a long time, away from us, from his own family. He has cooked for himself all these years." Marhamat had never forgiven herself for abandoning Hamed, letting him fend for himself in Tehran, all alone in a big, strange city.

Hamed blamed neither the war nor his move. Living in Tehran had given him a taste of independence, what it meant to be on his own, to do as he pleased. He had come to enjoy his life, experiencing the kind of autonomy that would be impossible back in his hometown. He was in no hurry to start a family of his own, to lose his precious freedom.

§

Leaving Moneer's parents' house, a peculiar dark silence wrapped Marhamat, Rahim, and Hamed, as if they walked in a vacuum. Hamed couldn't keep his thoughts focused. He ran a monologue in his mind, cataloguing all the flaws he had noticed—the dilapidated neighborhood, poorly decorated home, the long-winded mother with her unbearably high-pitched voice. *Daughters take after their mother, don't they?* he told himself acidly.

And the house itself! The living room was almost bare. The old sofa looked as if it had never been new; they hadn't even used a piece of cloth to hide the worn cushion. Was it yellow or green in its better days? He couldn't tell. A small plate of fruit was placed on a precarious coffee table. An opening space functioned like a dining area with a rickety metal table and four aluminum chairs.

Of course, Hamed was not concerned about money, but he did believe one doesn't have to be rich to have a beautiful house. There was not even a vase of flowers to make the occasion festive. How could that be? The plain, cheerless house looked depressing, dampening his enthusiasm after he had finally surrendered to Rahim's insistence on calling Moneer to arrange for a family visit.

It must be Moneer's mother, Mali Khanoom, who has no taste. A competent housewife wouldn't stand a house like that. As the thought flashed through his mind, a mild but wicked smile broke on his pursed lips—they should visit our house to learn a few things about housekeeping from my mother. He had an entire house to himself with all the rooms tastefully furnished by Marhamat.

Moreover, Hamed would have liked to have a word with Moneer's father, Mr. Hashemi, but Mali Khanoom didn't let the poor man utter a word. Hamed noticed Mr. Hashemi's sullen face and unfocused eyes. As he lowered himself on one of the metal chairs by the door, he looked like a shriveled green bean. Wordless and unexpressive, he had remained like this during the entire visit, with no sign of excitement or pleasure flickering in his blank eyes.

As Hamed felt assaulted by all these thoughts, he heard his father's voice.

"So, when would like to have the wedding? Your mother needs at least a month to prepare everything."

Turning to his father in disbelief, Hamed heard himself saying, "Father, I am not going to marry her." He tried hard to suppress the tremor in his voice.

"What do you mean?" Rahim asked.

"This was only an introductory gathering," replied Hamed indignantly.

"If you don't want to marry her, why did you want us to visit the family?"

"I just mentioned this girl to you a couple nights ago. I didn't mean we should pay them a formal visit."

"When you mention a girl, that means you're serious about her."

"I have met her only a few times at the office, but I didn't know anything about her or her family," Hamed said with a restrained voice. "She's a very quiet girl."

"Miss Moneer must be very bright, getting her doctorate," Rahim said as if he hadn't heard Hamed's reply.

"Yes, she's very smart. The only one in the family who went to college, but I am not marrying her, father!"

"You chose her!" Rahim said firmly this time.

"You saw them with your own eyes. They are a very traditional family." Hamed didn't want to say anything about how disappointed he was with their poor living conditions.

"Did you see Mali Khanoom's black chador? Even Moneer makes sure not even a strand of hair shows from under her scarf. I thought that's how she dresses outside, always covering herself from head to toe, always black, but she was like that even at her own home, as if we were total strangers."

"Well, we aren't that observant," said Rahim understandably. "But that shouldn't be a problem."

"Father, I am not interested in her," Hamed said angrily, "or her family."

"We met them for a purpose. They are a good, believing family," Rahim added with a stern voice. "We can't go back on our word. That wouldn't be honorable."

"We didn't give our word, father."

"Visiting them is the same as giving our word. They expect us to proceed. You should call them soon so we can make the proper arrangements before we leave."

§

As father and son talked, Marhamat kept to herself. Unfamiliar with Tehran, all she had noticed was that as the taxi got closer to the Hashemi's house, her heart sank deep in her chest. Stepping into their dim narrow hallway, it took her only a second to feel utterly dismayed. When they entered the living room, Marhamat immediately saw an older middle-aged woman with shrewd eyes placing serving plates strategically on a big dent with chipped paint on the metal dining table. Later the woman was introduced as Mali Khanoom's sister. As tea and cookies were served, Marhamat found herself fingering the chip on her saucer the whole time they exchanged pleasantries. While she held on to that cracked saucer, she didn't take a bite of her sweet. She couldn't swallow anything.

Marhamat had never lacked life's necessities, not even during the eight-year war with Iraq, the years of economic embargo and severe shortages of commodities. They didn't need to rely on government subsidies. Moreover, Rahim bought a beautiful house for Hamed when he moved to Tehran for college, and Marhamat decorated it on her own, purchasing all sorts of things. She had felt young, like a new bride, going from store to store, walking with her tall handsome son, buying furniture and kitchen items for Hamed. He was twenty-four and Marhamat and Rahim wanted to compensate for his years lost to the war, to ensure that he lived nicely. Over the years, Marhamat had showered Hamed with all he needed and more.

Torn between her son and Rahim, her daughter's advice echoing in her ears, Marhamat kept her distressing doubts to herself.

§

As Moneer's mother chattered away with her drilling, monotonous voice, others seemed to disappear behind their individual silence. Decisions had to be made—how many guests on each side? Where to hold the wedding? Which holy month? How many chairs and tables? What kind of side dishes to order and how many lamb kebabs? Who was going to buy the fruit? They had to be bought on the day of the wedding to ensure freshness. There were other concerns as well. Moneer's great aunt had to recuperate. No wedding would be held without her presence; not only a bad omen, it would be absolutely disrespectful.

The cost of the bride's gown? That could be negotiated. Yes, of course Moneer would move to Hamed's house after the wedding.

"Is your house ready?" Mali Khanoom inquired, turning pointedly toward Hamed. "You know my daughter is a real jewel for the man who steals her. She has always had the best in her life."

Noting the baffled look on her son's face, Marhamat came to his rescue by adding her own item to the list—"Flowers! We need flowers for the wedding. Tuberose and bird of paradise. And roses. White roses, I mean."

Hearing the heavy silence descending on the room, Marhamat forced a faint smile and continued, "One of our friends has a flower shop. He's been waiting for Hamed's wedding for a long time. He has promised to do the flower arrangements himself. He won't have his assistant do it. No, not for Hamed. He's like an uncle to my children."

Turning her entire heavy body toward Rahim who was sitting at the other end of the room, Mali Khanoom said loudly, "And the dowry," as if she had not even heard a word Marhamat said. "Let's not forget the most important thing." Looking at Rahim, she said proudly, "You know my daughter is getting her doctorate in literature."

"Of course, we'd be happy to oblige," Rahim said cordially, averting his eyes. "What do you have in mind?"

Without looking at Moneer, Mali Khanoom said, "You have married daughters and sons, and we respect your judgment. But given our daughter's higher education, we believe twenty-five *sekeh tala* (gold coins) is reasonable."

"We'll be happy to put sixty-five *sekeh tala* for Moneer Khanoom's dowry. Getting a Ph.D. is indeed an admirable endeavor. Our bride will bring more honor to our family with her doctorate," Rahim said with composure, a proud and satisfied expression covering his face. While Mali Khanoom fell silent for the first time, Moneer hastily got up to bring more tea, gliding across the room to hide her startled expression.

§

"But Father, why did you increase the dowry to sixty-five *sekeh*?" Hamed asked furiously the moment they stepped out of Moneer's house. "They asked for twenty-five, didn't they?"

"Son, we have to put forth the same dowry as your sister-in-law's," Rahim said positively. "We can't propose less."

"But they didn't ask for more," said Hamed furiously.

"They would find out about your sister-in-law's dowry sooner or later, and once they did, that'd be very bad for you. For the two families, for our brides," Rahim reasoned. "We can't start a relationship on bad faith."

Hamed remained upset but deep in his heart he agreed with Rahim's logic. It wasn't proper to assign a smaller dowry for his wife, especially because he was the oldest son.

§

It was Mali Khanoom's crowing that alarmed Hamed at the wedding after they were declared husband and wife. Congratulating her new son-in-law, she noisily kissed him on both cheeks, leaving a trace of her sweat on his cleanly shaven skin. Revealing a conniving smile, she said, "You know Moneer can cash in her dowry any time she wants to. From now on the dowry is hers!"

Taken aback, Hamed wasn't sure he had heard Mali Khanoom correctly in the middle of all the noise and commotion in the room. *Why cash in her dowry?* No woman in his family had ever come close to a divorce let alone cashing in her dowry. Even though it had not been his desire to marry at this point in his life, still, for Hamed marriage was a sacred union, and he couldn't think of any reason to break it. He believed a dowry was a symbolic gesture, an age-old tradition, perhaps a sign of respect the husband's family showed the young bride. Nothing more. In his mind, he had always thought respectable women should reject the entire notion because a dowry functioned as if women were for sale.

But in the coming days and months, Mali Khanoom kept reminding Hamed of Moneer's rights as a wife—the fact that the moment a marriage was consummated, the husband was held accountable for the full payment of the dowry. "She can cash in her dowry," had become her refrain. Hamed couldn't tell if she was just bantering or meant it as a threat. What he hadn't failed to notice was the mysterious grin that always accompanied the menacing comment. Hamed blamed the malicious repetitions on Mali Khanoom's annoying need to prattle. He had observed that her ceaseless chatter had silenced all the men in her family. Two years into the marriage, Hamed still hadn't exchanged a decent word with Mr. Hashemi. It was as if the poor man had no power of speech, except when the guests arrived and at the time of their departure. His small eyes set deep in his face spoke of a deep indifference.

§

Lost in his thoughts, Hamed was jolted when his office door sprang open and the man who served morning tea poked in his head. "Why is your door closed? I can't carry the tea tray and open the door at the same time," he complained loudly.

Staring blankly at the man, he merely replied, "Put the tea on my desk."

"Where else can I put it?" was the man's retort. "Mr. Imani was looking for you. I told him you weren't in yet."

"Why did you say that?" Hamed asked crossly.

"Your door was closed."

"So why are you bringing me tea if you thought I wasn't here?"

Hamed hadn't been able to bring himself to like the man who served tea.

"He has no manners," his colleagues had quietly complained to each other. Everybody agreed the tea man was a perfect example of a boorish person who showed no respect for authority. Nobody could touch him though. "He's a government spy," Hamed's colleagues said in a hushed voice amongst themselves. "He knows everything. Nobody can touch him."

"We don't have sugar cubes for tea today," he said before leaving Hamed's office.

Getting up from his desk, Hamed felt as if he was rising from under a ton of water. Habitually running his fingers through his light-brown hair, he looked out through his window. It was breakfast or maybe lunchtime for the sparrows and pigeons. Hundreds of them were loudly chirping under his window and in the big trees surrounding the old office building. Looking at the pigeons, he envied what he perceived as their tranquil existence. They walked across the yard, bobbing their heads continuously. Nothing seemed to disturb their harmonious movement for long. He had no idea how many of them had made those trees and the sides of the building their permanent home. Closing his window, he shut out their calming cooing. If they had made him smile before, they were now exacerbating his throbbing headache.

Hamed slowly walked toward his supervisor's office, clutching his notebook. Planting a placid smile on his pale face, he knocked on the door, announcing his presence while trying his best to hide the humiliating fact that his wife was plotting to divorce him after only three years of marriage. He was determined nobody should ever find out about it. *Absolutely nobody. What could be more shameful for a respectable man than being divorced?*

§

All day it had been painfully difficult for Hamed to stop himself from calling Moneer; supposedly he didn't know about this scandal. He wanted to go back to the night before, or the nights before that, willing to accept even the grave silence that had walled them from each other. *How selfish of Moneer to act so childishly.* But he had to conceal his maddening anger. It was time to teach a lesson in acting reasonably.

Having made up his mind, he decided that since Moneer didn't know Ayden had told him, he had time. It would take a couple of weeks for the court to send a letter.

I'll talk to her tonight, he told himself. He knew she'd come around. Everybody had told them they were a perfect couple. They had never experienced any serious problems, and minor arguments shouldn't be grounds for divorce or for cashing in a dowry.

Hamed planned his moves carefully. He pushed aside the distressing awareness that lately they had only talked at each other instead of to each other. He had found her increasingly withdrawn, even obstinate. The night before she was in her silent mood, going from room to room, opening and closing closets as if looking for something. Assuming she was still upset about their last disagreement, Hamed had kept to himself too. He knew Moneer usually resorted to days of silence after each trifling argument. They always disagreed over the most basic matters before and after having company. Moneer was reluctant to give dinner parties; she didn't enjoy entertaining Hamed's friends and relatives.

"It's a waste of money. And time," she had repeatedly said. "Why should we invite so many people all the time?"

"Because they have invited us," Hamed retorted. "We're just reciprocating their hospitality."

No longer interested in hiding his dislike of Moneer's family, he'd accused her, "The only people you want to have over are your family. Your parents, brother, sisters, aunts, and uncles. All that matters to you is your family. You care about them more than me, don't you?"

Moneer picked her fights, letting some comments hang in the air, as if they were not even voiced. While some topics were a constant source of tension between them, it wasn't easy to drag Moneer into a verbal confrontation, to get her to say what was on her mind. She usually withdrew right at the moment he could no longer control his temper, and that left him more furious with her, and mad at himself for losing his calm.

But some issues were permanent sources of contention. "How many dishes do you want to make for six people?" asked Moneer irritably every time they expected company.

"As many as possible. The more the better," Hamed countered. "We have to make as many dishes as they make. Maybe even more."

"That just doesn't make sense. With such high prices, we shouldn't be so wasteful."

But frugality was an insult to Hamed when it came to entertaining friends and family. His relations from the provinces visited and his parents came for short trips. If ten people came over for dinner, Hamed's mother cooked for thirty people. That was the proper way of entertaining. Anything less would reflect negatively on him. Moneer believed that was absurd.

Perhaps I am so overbearing that Moneer could no longer live with me. But what about aspiring for a better life? He disapproved of her housekeeping, of the way she entertained company, of her common manners. She served tea in unmatched cups and saucers. He hadn't had one cracked dish or saucer in his house, but after she had moved in everything seemed to develop cracks. Moneer didn't see the need to vacuum and dust the house for the company. She didn't even use the respectful form of addressing family elders. Hamed didn't like the way Moneer dressed either, never removing her dark black chador. The list of his dislikes was endless. He had concluded that people like her lived a confined life; they never came into contact with the outside world to learn about the finer things, such as dressing stylishly, trying new recipes, or decorating the house. Hamed had never forgotten how dismayed he was when he didn't see even a vase of flowers at Moneer's house the first time his family went to meet her parents. Not even red carnations—the kind of flowers people like her family would like. For Moneer flowers such as bird of paradise didn't exist. She didn't know that lilies came in spring, that a couple tuberose stems would fill the air with their calming scent in the heat of summer days. That tulips spoke to people, making heads turn, for they were really alive, dancing in their vase, arching their necks left and right as the light flirted with them. *No, Moneer and her folks are of a different kind of people. Not like us at all.*

§

Hamed had the taxi drop him off at the start of his street, intent on buying a few more minutes to better compose his thoughts, to rethink his strategy and the speech he was going to deliver about why Moneer should come back to her senses—if she had any—and act like a mature, responsible adult.

As Hamed got closer to the house, he noticed there were no lights on in the kitchen. Moneer was usually home by the time he arrived, having picked up their son Mohmmad from the daycare and already in the kitchen starting dinner. Struck by the darkness, he became all ears, trying to hear perhaps the TV, or Mohammad's chatter. Moneer was not interested in music, but she turned on the television for Mohammad while she worked in the kitchen.

He suddenly craved hearing his son's cheerful voice. Playing with Mohammad was the high point of his day, helping him forget all the problems of his clients. Mohammad had brought so much joy to his father's life, allowing Hamed to become a kid again, to play games his grandfather had played with him as a child. Their favorite fun was for Hamed to lie down on the floor on his back and bend his knees. Mohammad would climb up his dad's legs and sit on his feet while tightly holding his stretched hands. By raising his legs, Hamed brought Mohammad's small frame high in the air, and the child would laugh loudly. Hamed took him as high as he could, holding him up in the air while releasing one of his hands. They repeated this until Hamed finally unrolled on the floor, with Mohammad excitedly falling over him, both erupting into a thunderous laughter, which naturally drew Moneer out of the kitchen to make sure nobody was hurt.

But no noise drifted out of the dim kitchen window. Speeding up his steps, he almost tripped over the uneven pavement.

As he nervously unlocked the door, a grave-cold silence greeted him. It was about three years, yes, three years that he hadn't stepped into an empty house. Entering the hallway, he hesitated for a long moment, listening hard for any sound—a sigh, a whisper.

"Moneer? Mohammad *jan?*" he called out, barely recognizing his own trembling voice.

Cautiously walking to the kitchen, he touched the light switch, only to remember that the light bulb had died the night before. In the evening's gloomy shadow, he could see everything looked just as they had left it in the morning. The teacups and breakfast dishes in the sink, leftover bread and the honey container still on the kitchen table. Walking quietly upstairs to their bedroom, he told himself, Moneer is out grocery shopping. The fridge had been almost empty for a couple days.

Scanning the bedroom, Hamed wasn't surprised by the half-open wardrobe. Moneer didn't like to completely push in the drawers or close the doors, as if a fully closed drawer or bureau was beyond her.

"Does it take too much effort to properly close the closet door?" Hamed had asked several times.

"I need to put the clean laundry in the dresser," or "I need a fresh blouse," were her impatient replies as if it were none of his business. What shocked him was Moneer's obstinacy, her reluctance to change her ways about anything.

The wardrobe was completely stripped of its content, except for a few crooked rusty metal hangers that Moneer had brought with her. The vacant space looked violently exposed, like an old, unclothed woman.

He could not look away, barely able to breathe.

§

It was the loud ring of the phone that brought him back to reality. He couldn't tell how long he had sat at the edge of his bed, clutching a pillow tightly in his arms. He watched the phone as it kept ringing, it's red light arresting his attention.

"Hamed, Hamed *jan*," he heard his father's voice. "Where are you, dearest? We haven't heard from you in a long time!" Why don't you call your parents anymore? Give us a call, son, and let us hear your voice." His father sounded worried, but his concerned tone immediately became jovial as he mentioned Mohammad's name. "How's our delightful grandson? He's a grown man now, I'm sure! Your mother wants to talk to him. We both want to hear his voice. Call us, my son. Hearing your voice is our joy."

Noticing the long pause, Hamed painstakingly waited for his father's usual goodbye, "This is Rahim. Your father." As far as he could remember he had talked to them only a couple days ago.

To think his parents would ever find out about what Moneer had done was mortifying. *Nobody should ever find out about this. Nobody.*

§

When Hamed had returned from the war, he was a different man, having witnessed friends dying, their bodies blown into pieces. He had seen death in his best friend's eyes, still sitting straight up. He had learned that in war, death is a constant companion, always on the move, selectively choosing its momentary mates. Those who didn't die were nevertheless devastated by death's company. The younger the victim, the more delighted its cries of victory, the more eager to seek another innocent body. Hamed felt death escorted him day and night, calling to him, cajoling him, and sometimes engulfing him in a tight embrace. Hamed was certain he was next, but apparently death kept searching for more enticing conquests.

Returning alive from the war had been a victory against death. But life was no longer the same, as painless as everyone expected. Images of the war didn't leave him alone. Waking up in the middle of the night, he found himself soaked in sweat; he couldn't stop the noise in his head, the non-stop shelling, the joyous shrieks of death announcing continuous triumph.

The friend who had died in front of his eyes had always advised him to go to college once his service was over. "There is so much misery. So much poverty in this country. We need to do something," he had told Hamed in much anger.

As a son of jewelry shop owner who had never lacked anything in life, Hamed was struck by his friend's compassion for the poor. "But what can we do?" he asked. "We can't change the world. That's how the poor are. They aren't interested in changing their lives."

"No, no," his friend had cried out. "They are. But they don't know how to do it. They are born penniless and they live a destitute life because of lack of education. If you say that's how they are, then go and teach them better ways of living. Tell them they have to send their children to school, to college." Holding Hamed's hand firmly in his strong grip, he had continued passionately, "That's the only thing that can change their situation. The only thing."

"How can you do that? How can one teach the poor to live a better life? They won't even listen to you."

"Go to college. Study. You'll find a way."

Hamed was impressed by his friend's dedication, always repeating his advice to himself. He remembered his every word, his impassioned tone, his hunger for bettering the lot of the poor.

For months after his return from the war, all Hamed did, or was capable of doing, was rehearsing his friend's advice, "Go to college." Some of his old friends had left the country. One was going to college in Indonesia, another was working in Japan. He heard of Iranian communities in Turkey and India. People had also escaped to Western countries like Sweden and Germany. He dreamed about leaving the country too, to start all over, to leave behind war memories and images that haunted him day and night. He wanted to fly away.

One Friday, he visited his sister's family in Tehran. They had lunch at a restaurant. Noticing a young couple at the table sitting next to them, he felt captivated by the comfort, the ease with which they talked. When the platters of food came, he served her first, making sure she had everything on her plate before serving himself. In his family, his father was always the first to be served. As the young man served her girlfriend, their hands softly touched, coming together affectionately, and separating mindfully. He had never touched a girl's hand—at least not affectionately. The couple talked as if they were alone in that crowded noisy restaurant. Discreetly pulling his chair toward their table, Hamed eavesdropped.

"We'll move to Calgary. My sister will help us; I didn't want to tell you, but I've already talked to her," the young man said.

"But what about my coursework?" the woman asked, worry in her voice.

"No problem. You can transfer nine credits. Things will be much better in Calgary," he declared.

"It would be wonderful to live in a big city. Our town is so small. For heaven's sake, people turn their light off at 9:00 p.m.," the young woman said. Turning discreetly to supposedly adjust his chair, he noticed the woman's shiny eyes as if she was crying. "Where we are," she paused, "feels so lonely."

And that was the moment Hamed had a goal, a destination. He had no idea where Calgary was, but he was certainly going to find out. Yes, he was going to Calgary for college.

He told his mother about his plans.

§

"We are going to lose him again," Marhamat told Rahim the moment he was back from work.

"What do you mean? He's slowly getting his health back," Rahim said, sounding impatient with Marhamat's never-ending worries.

"Yes, but he wants to go away. To college," she said tearfully.

"There's nothing wrong with that," said Rahim. "We have a new university here. He's a war veteran. He can go to college right here. For free." Rahim knew war veterans had many privileges.

"No, he's talking about other countries. Places I have never heard about. A big city," Marhamat cried out.

"Where is he thinking about?" Rahim wanted to know.

"Who knows? We're going to lose him again."

Silence descended on the room where Rahim and Marhamat were sitting. For the past few months, Rahim had quietly walked to Hamed's bedroom at night, peeking in, watching his tormented face in sleep. He could tell Hamed was having nightmares by his constant moaning and the way he rolled and rolled in his bed. He could hear him waking up in the middle of the night, breathing hard as if he were choking. But Hamed never talked about the war. Rahim had never experienced war himself; his city was never bombed by Iraqi rockets. Rahim felt as if his son was still at the front, fighting the enemy in his sleep.

Tall and slim, Hamed had a non-imposing presence. His honey colored eyes looked as though he was always smiling. His soft voice was like a balm, manly and confident, but thoughtful and attentive as well. Growing up, he had been a source of joy for his parents, never causing worry. He was such a happy spirit before the war, Rahim thought. After the war, Hamed only stared into blankness, having lost his passion for life. Rahim would do anything for his son to enjoy life again. While Marhamat could hardly hide her fear of losing Hamed a second time, Rahim started thinking.

"It's not the end of the world. No need to cry," Rahim said confidently. "I'll think of something."

§

"Son, I need you to sign these papers," Rahim told Hamed, sounding serious, but smiling affectionately. "You're now my partner."

"But why, father?" said Hamed, clearly astonished to see the documents. "What are all these papers?"

"Whatever is mine is yours, son. This is a new deed for the shop. Everything I have belongs to you. I wanted to document that properly." He could barely hide his satisfaction.

Scanning the documents, Hamed said, "I don't know what to say, father, but I really can't accept this. This is extremely generous." Sitting on the couch, he read the pages of the document his father laid in front of him. Looking at his mother, who was silently standing by the door, Hamed noticed tears running down her face.

"Why don't you two relax," she said, "and I'll get some tea and sweets to celebrate?"

Rahim didn't tell Hamed to go to work. To open or close the store. He didn't show him where to buy his gold or which suppliers were trustworthy. He didn't ask him to be at the shop every day. He just gave him the newly drafted deed that documented his partnership. And the key. Hamed was no longer the son of a jeweler, but an owner in his own right.

Opening the shop became his daily task. He arrived at 9:30, opening the door at 10 sharp, sporting a nicely pressed shirt that Marhamat put out for him. Different masculine colors for different days of the week. There was always much traffic at the shop. He met young women who visited the store to try jewelry without any intention of purchasing. Perplexed by their behavior, he was totally indifferent to their hidden aspiration to perhaps find a jeweler husband or son-in-law. Or simply to try a nice gold ring for a few seconds, dreaming about it for days, envisioning the possibility of one day owning it.

Young engaged couples were accompanied by their parents and in-laws. Men brought their wives. Well-to-do women came alone or with a sister, maybe a friend, sometimes openly flirtatious, sometimes oblivious to his watchful presence. Nobody left their store without a smile, without the promise of returning after they made up their mind. Women who had saved their money for months, or perhaps years, came to buy gold as an investment; they wore their savings on their fingers, wrists, necks, showing off to friends and relatives. Hamed saw that Rahim let his good customers take the jewelry, try it a few days, and return it at no charge if they weren't happy with it. Or if their husband didn't approve of their purchase.

Rahim never wrote anything down; no receipts exchanged hands, for he knew his clients well.

Carefully observing the customers, Hamed soon came to distinguish the serious buyers from window-shoppers. He started to enjoy making a sale. He liked small groups of women who came to the store, trying a ring, perhaps a necklace. Putting on a necklace was the highpoint of the jewelry sale, whether or not the women bought anything. The gentle way they parted their veils, undoing the top buttons of their shirt collar to put on a necklace was a forbidden pleasure on both sides. Sometimes they couldn't clasp or undo the delicate lock and had to ask for his help. He obliged modestly, and courteously, without letting his fingertips touch the bare skin of the woman's neck. Averting his eyes, he could feel the heat of their bodies. He tried not to see the way they tilted their necks and pulled down the shirt a bit to get a better view of the necklace on their silky skin.

Hamed sensed the waves of energy floating in the shop. Sometimes he felt eager to open the store, greet the first group of customers. He always wondered how long it would take to make his first sale of the day. Quickly surveying the women, he could easily foresee how expensive a piece of jewelry they could afford. Watching his father, he quickly learned the secret tricks of the trade. If one or two women came in and asked to see a particular ring, Rahim pulled out two or three, strategically placing them on the counter while engaging in conversation with the supposed buyer. It usually took only a couple seconds for the non-buying customer to tentatively touch the ring, hesitantly trying it on her hand, and then put it back on the counter only to pick it up again. Once the women touched the gold, they were spellbound. Hamed knew he'd see the woman again in a few days, asking for the same ring Rahim had casually put in front of her.

Large groups of women, all heavily veiled, asking to see several rings or necklaces at the same time annoyed him. They were difficult to monitor. And they told him right to his face that his father was more competent and fairer than him. Staring boldly at him, they dared him to reply. He preferred the young bashful girls who accompanied their mother and were too shy to look at him directly. They only stole glances while checking the jewelry, watching their mothers as they tried a necklace or a ring. He found their taste more appealing. Unlike their mothers, they looked for beauty in the gold rather than the weight of the piece.

As Hamed continued working at the shop, the image of the young couple at the restaurant lost color. He had difficulty remembering the name of the city they mentioned. *What was it?* He remembered it started with a C. Cula, maybe a G, Galua? No, no, it was a C. Forgetting the proper name of the city troubled him. Tossing and turning in his bed at night, he willed himself to remember the name by morning. *I will remember it. It will come to me.* But he woke up in the morning still having no clue what the city was called.

Preoccupied with running the store properly and proving that he deserved his father's trust, his nightmares became less frequent. But his friend didn't leave him alone, often appearing in his sleep, repeating his advice. "Go to college. Help the poor." Perhaps the never-ending stream of customers and their lust for gold finally exhausted him. Perhaps the memory of his friend was too strong. Perhaps his heart wasn't really into being a salesman after all. Sometimes he would look at the mirrored wall, and he'd see his friend staring at him angrily.

"What are you doing here?" he'd ask sharply.

"This is my shop. I work here," Hamed would respond sheepishly.

"Didn't you promise to go to college? To study?"

"I didn't. I mean, I did, but now I am here. I have this store to run," Hamed would reply apologetically, as if he were a traitor.

"Poor people need you. If you don't help them, who will, my friend?"

Unable to explain or justify his delay in going to college, Hamed watched his friend with horror as he calmly stepped out of the mirrored wall, opened the shop door, and pointed to a beggar woman who sat on a piece of cardboard across the street, selling matches and a few packages of gum. She was there at the same spot every day.

"Look with your own eyes," he'd turn, looking at Hamed sternly. "She needs you. Her children need you. If you don't help her, her grandchildren will be doing the same thing. Sitting on a street corner summer and winter, day and night, selling chewing gum. There is no hope for people like her without you."

§

When Hamed was admitted to the university, he didn't know how to tell Rahim. It was again Marhamat who gave her husband the news.

"Hamed is going to college," Marhamat said. Rahim's pause was so long that she wasn't sure he heard her. "In Tehran. He is going to Tehran for college," Marhamat said again.

"That's good news," Rahim finally said after a long pensive silence. "That shows he's getting better. Perhaps he is at last recovering," he said, trying to sound positive. "Besides, all his cousins have gone to college. It's good for him," thoughtfully nodding his head.

Once more, it was Rahim who travelled to Tehran unexpectedly, returning in a few days with a new folder in his hands. Putting a thick envelope on Hamed's bed, he awaited his return from the shop.

§

Unlike many of the students from the provinces, Hamed didn't stay at the dorm or rent a room at a stranger's house. He moved straight to the home Rahim had bought for him. Leaving behind his family, the jewelry shop and all of the women who frequented it, Hamed was motivated once again. Losing years to the war and his subsequent depression, he was intent on finishing his degree as quickly as possible, pleased about finally fulfilling his promise to his friend.

He took more than a full load of classes, worked at the private office of his advisor, Mrs. Kamrani, for long hours, helping with her research on autistic children. He often worked alone far into the night, studying or researching for a paper. Everybody was impressed by his progress, by how rapidly he was finishing his degree, working tirelessly on several projects simultaneously. Hungry for reading, Hamed soon became a walking library. Others learned to come to him for help.

§

Proofreading his supervisor's paper, he sensed the presence of a woman. The rustling sound of a woman's veil. Looking up from his work, he was taken aback by a woman, clad all in black, standing by his office door. Just as their eyes locked, she averted her gaze.

"I am here to see Professor Kamrani," the woman said tentatively.

"She's not in today," Hamed replied curiously, trying to hide his surprised smile.

"I have an appointment today at 9:30," the woman said, sounding clearly disappointed. "Are you sure she's not coming in today?"

"Well, she just called and said she'll be in a meeting all morning."

Rising from his chair, he asked, "Is there anything I can do for you?"

"I need a copy of one of her articles," she said. "For my research."

"I'd be happy to make another appointment for you," Hamed said courteously. Checking his supervisor's calendar, he asked nonchalantly, "Your name?"

"I have talked to Professor Kamrani on the phone," the woman said, "she knows me." A long pause came as she gave Hamed a discreet but appraising look. "Are you sure she's not coming today?"

He liked her assertiveness. "I just talked to her and she instructed me to cancel all her appointments for the day."

"Well, okay, I can come back tomorrow the same time," she said, turning on her heel.

"Let me see. There is an opening tomorrow at 11:30 …?" Hamed heard himself talking into a void.

§

Was he acting deviously, he didn't know, but he made sure he was at the office the next day the woman came. Asking his supervisor about the woman's project, he went out of his way to find related articles. Hamed was clearly older, more experienced, and he had conversed with many women at the shop. Not only was he not shy about striking up a conversation with a woman, he also knew how to look deep into her eyes, how to hold her gaze, and when to glance away.

He energetically dove into a game with his seemingly innocent prey. When she came a third time, he acted warmly but respectfully. After her meeting with Professor Kamrani, he politely asked if she had a few minutes, eager to show her the articles he'd found, suggesting new pieces. He had her stop by the office again, offering valuable help, promising new books and translations, referring to obscure pieces he was trying to unearth while allowing ample opportunity for her to examine him, to observe him, to access his information. Hamed was full of promises. He was sure the woman would fall for his overtures veiled in academic help.

Carefully working on courteously offering scholarly advice, Hamed slowly and unknowingly fell into the fine net of attraction and seduction he was weaving. Moneer had remained a closed entity, purely interested in her academic pursuit. She had not returned his friendly overtures, and refused to hold his gaze. His playfulness was treated with polite but cold indifference. She came right on time for her scheduled appointments, engaged in minimal talk, and left immediately after their exchange was complete. Never lingering a moment longer nor asking a non-academic question to initiate a friendly conversation. The more aloof she acted, the more intense Hamed's interest. But Moneer's clothing intimidated him; she was always fully covered, even using a dark head scarf under her black chador. There was never a hint of immodesty about her, not even a single strand of hair peeking from under her tight scarf and veil. Not even a faint inviting smile. Hamed was fully aware that she'd never agree to visit him outside his adviser's office. If other young couples strolled in the park, a walk with Moneer seemed like an impossibility.

The man who believed he was in control never thought he'd be at a loss. No amount of charm or academic help brought Moneer into his web. Hamed had become his own victim, mistakenly assuming his charm, wit, and academic attention would finally melt away Moneer's resistance. Instead it was he who was captivated by the young woman he didn't know. The more reserved she acted, the more eager Hamed became, admiring her piety and virtue. He was the one who began divulging facts of his private life. He had mentioned his home, his family, his years of work experience at his father's jewelry shop. Even then she had maintained her distance, never giving him a chance to entertain the possibility of a friendship, even a platonic one if such a relationship ever existed.

Reaching a dead-end, Hamed had turned to his father, believing he couldn't advance any further. But it didn't take long to realize his mistakes in involving Rahim and in recognizing Moneer was nothing like he'd believed she was. When Hamed recognized his mistakes, his father had brutally told him, "You chose her."

Father

Somebody was out there, banging on the door. Who was there at this ungodly time of the night?

Rubbing his neck, Ali looked anxiously toward the bed. Layla was lying there, breathing slowly. She was finally home. They hadn't told anybody about the first miscarriage, but this one was too close; she had almost lost her life. He had skipped work to stay by her bedside.

Bang, bang on the door. Who was out there? Ali wasn't going to open it. Not on a night like this. Heavy snow had driven everybody to their homes. All the stores were closed; most people didn't dare step out of their houses. Work had come to a halt in the city.

It was a brutally cold winter, the kind of cold that was unprecedented in the entire country. No heater was able to fight the subfreezing temperatures. People had started covering their doors and windows, staying in one room while the rest of the house turned into an open freezer. Their breaths looked like chimney smoke.

As if the situation was not bad enough, there were shortages, long lines, and pernicious anxiety about the latest unpredictable policy change by the government. Now the entire city was besieged by this unbearable cold. The government had appealed to warmer provinces to use less gas in order to provide enough for the colder regions. After the revolution, the government had promised that natural gas would be free for all. Only promised.

Bang, bang, bang. They'll go away; nobody can stay out in this cold for too long, Ali growled to himself.

Before her miscarriage, Layla had begun wearing woolen gloves at home, but nothing could keep her warm. She needed her rest and quiet. After days, Ali noticed that she was finally breathing quietly, as if her body was gradually coming back to life. He saw her hands moving slightly, perhaps unconsciously, touching the soft sheets. She had always loved to touch everything, to get a feeling of how things felt against her skin.

Ali hadn't left her side for days. More than anything else, he wanted Layla to be healthy. He wanted her to be his lively, vivacious wife again: the woman who had stolen his heart.

§

Ali's parents had been overjoyed with the news of his engagement to Layla. They couldn't wait for the wedding. Even though he was the eldest son, Ali was the last one to marry. Tradition was that older siblings should marry first. So his brothers had long ago pleaded with Ali:

"When are you going to marry?"

Later, the youngest one had asked: "How long do you think I have to wait till I can marry?"

Ali was caught completely by surprise. He had no idea his younger brothers were so in love that they were thinking about marriage. So Ali had pleaded with his parents to overlook family tradition and cultural expectations. He convinced them to agree to his younger brothers' marriages before his. He told them it was all right to be modern when it came to matters of love. He was the eldest, the wisest, the most rational, and the most responsible and dependable. He had cared for his younger siblings when they joined him after his move to Tehran for college. Their parents stayed put in their hometown with the younger children. Moving back home was not an option for Ali; he had seen a different world in Tehran, met different people, got a nice job after graduation, and bought a nice little place, where he housed his brothers. He had done all that in a short time, and he was a symbol of triumphant success in his parents' eyes.

When Ali told his parents he had met the right woman, a co-worker, they could no longer wait. Who was this woman who had finally succeeded in attracting their son?

They told him they would do anything for him and the woman he loved. They promised to buy her the most expensive jewelry, accept her into their family, and shower her with all the love they had. They told him that Layla would have her own superior place in the family as the wife of their eldest son, in spite of her late arrival. Ali's parents were traditional, but they still had tremendous love for their eldest son, who had separated his path from them at the age of eighteen to go to college. He was their source of pride and delight. Ali was the kind of son that any girl back in his hometown would long to marry. He had taken his time in finding the woman he loved.

§

Ali brought Layla home, driving carefully in spite of the crazy traffic. Holding her gently, he led her to the bedroom, and helped her sit down on the bed. He noticed a teardrop finding its way down her cheek, and gently brushed it off with the back of his hand. Was it physical exhaustion or emotional pain? He didn't know.

Arranging pillows behind her, he softly helped her lean back, pulling the wool blanket over her weakened body. He thought about placing extra pillows at her sides for more comfort and warmth. The loss seemed to have drained her; he went to the kitchen to make tea, knowing that she wouldn't be able to eat much.

The snow had started to fall again. He always listened to the sound of silence when it snowed, and this silence brought news of more snow to come. When he was a child, he marveled each morning when he woke to see the yard dressed up in white. It was as if nature had given a white garden party the night before. As a child, he sat behind the window, trying to listen to the snowflakes waltzing till they embraced one another, nestling on tree branches and becoming one with the branch. He was amazed at how many words his parents' language had for different kinds of snow.

§

In a city that never stopped, there were now no cars in motion. There were no street sweepers cleaning the streets with their long brushes early morning. Tired and drained, Ali realized he hadn't eaten all day.

Resting the warm cup of tea on the pillow Ali had placed on her lap, Layla slowly sipped the sweetened tea, closing her eyes between sips. Thankful to see Layla's cheeks picking up color, Ali remained by her bed, examining her every move, watching her breathe. He touched her slender hands, softly caressing them. Feeling her hand tightening its grip had an immediate calming effect on him.

Bang, bang on the door again. Reluctantly, he pulled himself up from his wooden chair, and tugged the curtain aside a tad to look through the foggy window. He squinted against the blinding whiteness and saw two silhouettes: a tall, slim man and a woman standing against the streetlight. She was trying to hide her face against the blizzard and the violent wind. A small bag rested at her feet on a pile of snow. She had wrapped herself in layers to protect against the icy snow that slowly covered her entire body. The man now relentlessly banged on the door. Running to the door, Ali almost lost his balance.

There they are, Ali whispered to himself. A big smile covered his tired face. *They have come.* He hadn't talked to them for a few days, but they should have known something was wrong. As the door opened, his father couldn't wait to hold him tight in his arms. As he embraced Ali, he promised all would be well. They had come. He knew they would never leave him alone. He could count on his parents, even without asking for help.

Author Bio

MAHNAZ KOUSHA IS a professor of sociology at Macalester College in Saint Paul, Minnesota. She focuses on the intersection of gender, race, class and family relationships in her teaching and research. She is the author of *Voices from Iran: Changing Lives of Iranian Women*. She has co-translated the novel, *My Bird*, by Fariba Vafi. As a co-founder of *Critique: Journal for Critical Studies of the Middle East*, she has served on its board of directors.

CPSIA information can be obtained
at www.ICGtesting.com
Printed in the USA
LVOW12s2228150518
577261LV00003B/574/P